THE GREEN DOOR

THE GREEN DOOR

A Novel

Lennon Nersesian

iUniverse, Inc.

New York Lincoln Shanghai

THE GREEN DOOR

iUniverse books may be ordered through booksellers or by contacting:

iUniverse
2021 Pine Lake Road, Suite 100
Lincoln, NE 68512
www.iuniverse.com
1-800-Authors (1-800-288-4677)

This is a work of fiction. All of the characters, names, incidents, organizations, and dialogue in this novel are either the products of the author's imagination or are used fictitiously.

ISBN: 978-0-595-43748-1 (pbk)
ISBN: 978-0-595-88077-5 (ebk)

Printed in the United States of America

PROLOGUE

My heart was pounding.

An odd sensation for someone who died yesterday, I thought, forcing an unconvincing chuckle. *But then again, if there were ever a time for a dead man's heart to beat, this would be it.*

I sheepishly stepped into my grandparents' decaying shed for the first time since that horrific night thirty-two years ago, knowing that all of those memories of that stormy night, which I systematically hid in the cul-de-sac of my subconscious, would soon flood over me like water from a busted gasket.

There is no turning back now. There are no more choices.

It was time to escape the safety and comfort of heaven to wrestle my wrongfully condemned brother away from the darkest chasm of hell.

The shed door creaked shut behind me.

My adventure began.

1

THE END

As the dueling club heads banged in the backseat of my '87 white convertible Cabriolet to the beat of the percussion track laid down by the road bumps, complementing the distant bassy rumbles of thunder as if playing a game of musical *Simon Says* with Mother Nature's impending storm, providing the only alternative to the broken radio—save from spontaneous disharmonious duets of Beatles' songs between my younger brother Rob and me—I wondered how many strokes I would have to relinquish to absolve my guilt.

Rob was never much of a golfer, but he was most certainly always a competitor. Whether it was in street hockey, wiffle ball, or golf, we would usually end our childhood competitions with a nasty amalgamation of blood and tears. We made billiards a contact sport. Sword fights with pool cues in our grandparents' basement determined who would break.

Although we were much older as my Cabriolet transported us down a desolate highway toward a weekend of golf, we taunted, compared, and joked about each other's game like a pair of children, like carefree brothers.

Rob finally succumbed, reclined the passenger's seat, and fell asleep.

Golf was always my sport, but it had been years since Rob and I battled, and although I was victorious in the verbal sparring, I feared that he was better prepared for the real battle that was to follow.

This time there was to be no "human drama of athletic competition" where one would rub the thrill of victory into the agony of the other's face. For the first time, I would get no pleasure beating my brother on the course.

As I glanced over at Rob sleeping, I was once again twelve, and my brother eight, and although we never got to finish our last round together at that young impressionable age, I was determined not to allow that to happen again.

◆   ◆   ◆

Rob and I were playing at the exclusive Rockland Country Club with our father. Our neighbor, who was a highly influential and charitable member at the time, invited us to take his tee time while he was away on business. It was the perfect stage for our much anticipated 'mono y mono' brotherly death match where everything would be laid on the line.

Or so I thought.

Even though our neighbor warned our dad of the country club's prejudice toward children, he promised he would take care of everything so we wouldn't have any problems.

I felt uncomfortable from the moment we had to valet our car, and that feeling only amplified when the greenskeeper told us to tuck in our collared shirts before approaching the first hole.

"There is a very strict time limit," the greenskeeper warned my dad. His eyes were locked on Rob as we paid the green's fee. For some reason, I didn't feel like we were welcome, and I had the strange sensation that we were being eyeballed the entire day.

My middle school team played at a nearby weed-infested public course where replacing divots and raking sand traps were only polite suggestions, not amendments to the ten commandments. This was my first authentic golfing experience; I was confused, excited, and suspicious. I had no other intention than to play by the course rules, respect the game, and teach my brother a much-needed lesson in golfing subservience 101.

Dad reluctantly assumed the position of referee. His major concern was to make sure that our round didn't turn into a fencing match. Or worse yet, one of our billiards competitions. I also knew that Dad would compete hard and not shy away from taking home bragging rights.

However, according to the rules, he was disqualified before he teed up his ball on the first hole. Dad did not associate walking with golf. He did, however, associate driving a cart with the century old game. Maybe because I was young and vibrant, or maybe because being on my school golf team taught me how to play the game as it should be played, I always refused to hitch a ride.

"Not only is it good exercise, walking also helps your game because it forces you to take your time in-between shots," I tried to explain to my obstinate father, as the starter handed him the keys to his golf cart.

"You're cheating," I'd shout out. "It's like a baseball player using steroids."

All arguments were futile, especially after he'd take a dose of Percocets or Vicodins before the first hole to counteract a day of anticipated physical abuse. It didn't really matter to me anyway. This was a competition between my brother and me. Dad could practice his parallel parking next to a bunker or his K-turns through a set of trees in the rough.

Rob didn't see how walking the course added to the 'purity of the game' either because he wouldn't stop badgering Dad to let him drive.

Course rules, however, clearly stated that guests must be twenty-one to drive the carts. I always found that quite peculiar, being that at sixteen years of age, a driver's license is easily and legally accessible, but rules were rules, a saying my brother never really took to heart. I guessed a more appropriate adage for my eight-year-old brother was, 'rules are made to be broken'. And so are wooden fences, which was exactly what my little brother proved when my dad finally gave in to his incessant pleading.

Rob must have been so excited to have been given the opportunity to drive the golf cart a stimulating total of twenty feet at a scintillating speed of twelve miles an hour that he forgot to take his foot off the gas. I watched from the seventeenth green my brother and my father drive straight through a wooden fence before crashing into a tree past the eighteenth tee box.

Despite all of the smoke, I knew nobody was hurt because I immediately heard both accident victims laughing uncontrollably at their folly. Before I could react, a nubile park ranger, wearing more pimples on his face than hair, came running from the seventeenth fairway in his tennis shoes and knee-high socks while waving his arms above his head to flaunt his premature authority.

I had noticed that very same park ranger following us from hole to hole on the front nine, but I didn't think anything of it. I was too busy out-driving and out-scoring my brother to begin concocting crazy country club conspiracies.

The untrusting country club snobs, who were both managers and members of the course, probably didn't trust two 'punk' kids on the loose with crooked sticks on their million-dollar property disrespecting the game. He was their spy.

God forbid we have any fun.

They were looking for any excuse to throw us off the course, and because Rob didn't know the difference between a golf cart's brake pedal and accelerator pedal, a system scarcely more advanced than the pedals in a battery-powered *Fisher Price* toy car, they got their excuse.

I told you, carts ruin the game.

"Nobody move," the ranger commanded, as he made his way over to the damaged golf cart and its giddy inhabitants. "How old are you, son?"

"I'm twenty-three but short," my brother blurted out.

My face turned white. *He's going to get us banned*, I thought. *I'll never be able to play golf here again.*

The one lesson that my golf coach taught me was that private golfing establishments have zero tolerance for guests who show disrespect towards their course.

If I hide behind a cluster of bushes, I planned, *the park ranger won't know I'm with the two troublemakers.*

I prayed that Dad would take control of the situation.

"He refuses to eat broccoli so his mother and I mix Insta-Grow fertilizer in his breakfast cereal," my father sneered. "Our doctor says he'll reach the normal height for his age group within the year. Unfortunately, one of the side effects is he'll never be able to play the piano."

He was provoking an argument, and here I had thought my Dad would side with the uniformed stranger and later condemn my brother to a weekend of no television and no allowance for the careless crash.

The ranger, his face turning red, raised his hand, as if it were a fiery scythe, high above Rob's trembling face. "You're coming with me," he scowled.

"Hey, take it easy. We were just kidding around," Dad said nervously, realizing that the ranger meant business. "It was an accident."

As I hid behind the bushes, I imagined a red tail would soon maturate from the enraged park ranger before he'd effectuate a world of fire to the powerless golfing sinners. Instead, he forcefully grabbed Rob's arm and squeezed it tight.

I could tell Rob was scared. So was I.

"Get your hand off him," Dad said, this time with more conviction.

The ranger, with malicious intent in his eyes, was hurting Rob badly. He began tugging at his arm. I thought he was going to pull it right out of his socket. "Let's go you little shit," the ranger yelled.

Rob began crying.

Why isn't Dad doing anything?

As if my unspoken question was suddenly transported telepathically to my indecisive father, he finally took action. Dad grabbed at the ranger's wrist and yanked his arm off Rob's who sat behind the wheel of the golf cart in stunned silence.

"I said, get your hand off him," Dad snapped, pulling the ranger's arm closer to him so he could better extinguish the fire in the monster's eyes.

He had the park ranger on the defensive. "By the way, do you mind fixing my divot?" Dad asked rhetorically. He was now taunting the devil right to his face.

"What divot?" The devil was confused.

I couldn't tell for certain from behind the bushes, but I thought I saw my Dad smile and wink at the park ranger before gripping the wheel and stepping on the accelerator. The startled ranger was caught off-guard. The wheels spun hysterically, tearing up the eighteenth fairway, as Rob and Dad sped toward me.

I'm involved now.

They stopped in front of the bushes and beckoned for me to jump on the back of the cart. I was so scared. I didn't know what to do. I wished I could have just hid behind those bushes forever.

"Hurry up," Dad pleaded. "Get on."

The park ranger was now closing in on the cart. I noticed the terror in Rob's eyes. I had to act fast. Without wasting another precious moment, I seized my golf bag, scampered out of the bushes, and hopped onto the back of the cart. "Go," I screamed, as I clutched my bag tightly with my sweaty hands. I was within the ranger's grasp. He extended his arms. "Drive!"

Dad slammed on the gas just before the ranger could get to us, and we were off, down the side of the eighteenth fairway, Rob, stunned in silence, Dad, driving perilously from the passenger's seat, and me, hanging on for dear life on the open back of a moving vehicle, making our getaway in a crumpled golf cart at a robust twelve miles an hour.

As our distance from the park ranger grew from a seven iron to a five iron shot, I finally knew we would be safe. I could tell by the look on the ranger's face that he decided not to pursue.

As we passed an aghast foursome on the eighteenth green, all I could think about was the amount of course violations we were currently breaking. I chuckled and exhaled in relief.

That night, as I lay silently on the top of my brother's bunk bed replaying the afternoon's incident again and again in my head, I couldn't help but to feel an overwhelming deference for my father. It didn't matter whether my brother was wrong for crashing the golf cart or not, my Dad wasn't going to let anybody harm his own blood. I learned a valuable lesson about the meaning of family. *No matter what I do or who I become, I can always come home.*

I returned to the country club a few months later with my golf team, and as my group approached the eighteenth tee box, I noticed that one of the boards comprising a nearby fence was less weathered than the rest. I decided to tell my teammates the story behind the supplanted two-by-four.

I stared at the board for a number of seconds and smiled.

Dad always told us to always leave our mark.

◆   ◆   ◆

Either we were approaching the storm or the storm was approaching us because I noticed the rainfall strengthening. *I hope it doesn't rain for our weekend of golf.* I glanced over at Rob who continued to sleep, his jacket serving as a makeshift blanket. I was bored. The percussion of the rattling golf clubs in the backseat was no longer music to my ears.

Should I wake him? I could use a good conversation.

However, at the time, I didn't know any better, so I let him sleep.

Boredom quickly gave way to tiredness as rain gave way to downpour.

Damn broken radio.

There weren't any other cars on the road to keep me company and it was too dark to enjoy the passing scenery. As if having seen enough, I felt the weight of my eyelids momentarily succumb to gravity, cloaking my somnolent hazel green eyes. "Don't fall asleep," I told myself.

I blasted the air conditioning in my face, hoping the cool breeze would recharge my system and give me a much-needed second wind. *Maybe I should ask Rob to drive the rest of the way.* I glimpsed over at Rob who must have reached REM sleep by now, and even though I would have loved to wake him from his non-productive state and force him to drive the last leg of our road trip, I didn't want to disturb him more than I already had.

A bolt of lightning streaked across the sky. *One one hundred, two one hun …*

An explosion of thunder shook the car.

How could Rob sleep through that blast? I wondered.

For as long as I could remember, Rob never slept through a thunderstorm. He was too busy screaming his head off, pleading with Mom to hang up the phone, and racing around the house to power down all of the lights and TVs before we were the one in a million chance of being struck by a bolt of lightning inside the house. And, as if he still didn't feel safe enough, Rob would then go down to the garage and sit in the car for the duration of the storm with his hands over his ears.

Cars are the safest place to take refuge in when it's lightning out, I remembered my sixth grade earth science teacher lecture.

◆   ◆   ◆

The ballgame was saturated with drama, just like the impending weather system overhead. Full count. Bases loaded. Tie score. Bottom of the ninth inning. The pitch of the game was about to ensue, and the game ball was in the hands of my brother.

Little League at its finest.

Rob changed his grip on the baseball, nodded to the catcher as he checked the idle base runners, and set at the belt. I didn't know whether the high pressure system on the field or the one in the sky would precipitate first. Both were inevitable.

Just as Rob began his delivery, the heavens opened up and a bolt of lightning illuminated the sky. The light bulb in Rob's head must have shorted out because he stopped himself mid-windup, let out a high-pitched scream, and sprinted off the mound, much to the delight and wonderment of the fans.

I knew exactly where he was going. The car.

Rob sprinted across the field, hopped the left-field fence, and locked himself inside the family sedan. The bases remained loaded. The count still full. But now, the pitcher with the game ball was hiding in the backseat of a car with his hands over his ears shaking fearfully with each rumble of thunder.

Great person to trust with the game on the line.

"Well, at least there are no balks in this league," I heard one fan joke, as we all congregated under a nearby tree to wait for the storm to pass.

Rob's coach walked through the storm and waited beside the car for his ace pitcher to show his face. If he did, then the dissipating thunderstorm would have been the least of his problems. He had two teams of nine year olds waiting to tease and torment the scaredy-cat pitcher from their respective dug-outs.

"Come on, son," the coach repeated for forty-five minutes. "We need you. Do you know what the odds are of getting struck by lightning?"

All attempts at coaxing my brother back to the mound to finish the game were futile. Ben Frye, a bench player who would scream out, "Spoon," whenever a ball was hit to him during the mandatory allotted three defensive outs he had to play in games, replaced Rob on the mound after the rain delay, and immediately gave up a game losing double. Rob never left the backseat of the car.

I never let him hear the end of it.

◆   ◆   ◆

I had my share of phobias, too. Clowns and dogs were two in particular that got my adrenaline bubbling. When I was six years old, I went with my friend, Laura, and her mom, Diane, to get their car washed. I loved going through the car wash. Every time I'd try to imagine partaking in some sort of adventure as the car got cleaned.

On that particular day, I was on a spaceship battling aliens. The scrubbers buffing the sides of the car were my enemies and the soap they sprayed onto the windows was their weapons. Just as I was steering my intergalactic craft to safety, I was jolted back into reality at the disturbing sight of Batman and the Joker waving us out of the darkened car wash and into the light of day.

The car pulled to a stop in front of the superhero and his arch enemy. Laura was excited to see them. "Can we take a picture with Batman and the Joker?" she cried.

I didn't share her enthusiasm.

The Joker, holding a yellow balloon, made his way over to my window. He knelt down, smiled, and tapped on the glass. "Want a balloon?" he asked.

I stared fearfully into the clown's wicked eyes. *Don't open the window. Don't open the window*, I willed.

Diane opened the windows. I was helpless as my descending glass shield exposed me to the monster. I wanted to ride the window right into the safety of the car door. Laura clapped happily. I screamed my head off. I probably scared the Joker more than he scared me. My shrieks and my subsequent hyperventilation drew quite a bit of attention. A small crowd had surrounded the car, and they weren't admiring its newly applied shine. Batman attempted to quell my hysterics by killing the Joker with a phantom punch to the gut. But, he didn't fool me. Not a child who had just saved the planet against bloodsucking aliens from the planet Krudor.

Laura, embarrassed, pulled her shirt over her face as Diane failed to calm me down with her encouraging words.

I kept repeating, "I want to go home!"

Diane finally relented. We drove home in silence, Laura never getting her picture with the Caped Crusader and his most infamous villain.

From that day forward, I refused to attend any birthday party that had clowns as a source of entertainment.

Years later, after I had thought I grew out of my silly childhood fear of clowns, I would be plagued by a recurring nightmare of a killer clown following me around at a circus.

"It's amazing what comes back from the past to haunt you," I'd tell myself.

It was harder to pinpoint where my fear of dogs began, but for as long as I could remember, I was running away from them. I could be among a large group of people, and dogs would single me out of the crowd as the one to chase and torment.

"They can smell your fear," people would tell me.

They can smell my fear, I ironically feared. That was a scary thought.

Many of my friends growing up had dogs. I would make them tie their dogs up outside or lock them in an unoccupied room whenever I visited. My excuse was, "I'm allergic to them. I bleed when their teeth pierce my skin."

One afternoon, Rob and I were riding our bikes back from a candy/pizza trip into town, and as we reached the top of a hill, a dog, probably sensing my malodorous odor of fear, escaped a nearby fence and dashed in our direction. I only heard its barking so I didn't know whether we were dealing with a 200 pound rabid pit bull or a miniature poodle named Snowflake. It didn't matter to me. I sped down the hill on my bike, much to the amusement of my brother, in a staggering state of consternation. I could sense the dog right on my trail. The sound of its panting and barking were closing in on my back wheel.

This monster can run like the wind.

I sped up, the pedals spiraling out of control, my feet failing to keep up. I faintly heard Rob laughing from the top of the hill, but my thoughts were too consumed with my assailant to rebuke his relentless jests. I imagined my four-legged beast foaming at the mouth and showing off its sharp vampire fangs as it prepared to pounce on my sixteen speed multi-terrain two wheeler, taking me down like a hot-tempered mountain lion on a 'wrong place at the wrong time' forest elk.

My bike was teetering out of control, and just as I made it to the bottom of the hill, I lost balance and violently cannon-balled to the asphalt, cutting my knee and completely wrecking my bike in the process. Now vulnerable to a ground attack, I braced myself for a Cujo-like encounter.

One second passed. Two seconds. At that moment, the passage of time was my greatest ally because it signified that I was still alive.

What is that licking sensation?

I gathered enough courage to face my fear. I opened my eyes to witness a miniature terrier affectionately licking the bloody gash on my knee. I finally acknowledged the absurdity of my phobia and my uncanny ability to overreact and cause an embarrassing scene. Rob skidded to a stop in front of my disjointed bike, scaring the whimpering puppy back up the hill, and erupted into a frenzied laughter.

He never let me hear the end of it.

I quickly realized that I would have to mask my redolent fears with much more pleasant aromas or else I'd be attracting and running from my nightmares for the rest of my life.

You never know whom or what is picking up on a foul scent.

Even though I had eventually learned to co-exist with man's best friend, I still preferred cats ... or goldfish.

I had thought I cured my phobias for good, and maybe I succeeded at extinguishing my frivolous fear of dogs and clowns, however, as I would learn, there were bigger, more evil, and less defined threats to my physical and mental stability that have a keener sense of smell than most normal predators that feed on fear. Not even the most fragrant of colognes could misguide them off my trail, especially when they had spent a lifetime under my nose and in my subconscious unknowingly paving the aforementioned trail for me.

◆   ◆   ◆

Lightning.

One one hun ...

A deafening crackle of thunder signified our unwelcome admission into the epicenter of the storm. A sonic boom. Again, Rob did not wake.

We passed a sign, possibly divine, carrying a message that read, "Last exit for 30 miles." I contemplated getting off so I could pull over and rest my eyes for a few minutes, but with a little less than one hour left to the Marriott, according to Mapquest, I decided otherwise.

There's no turning back now.

I could tell that Rob was getting cold under his jacket. I shut off the air conditioning and re-activated the defroster. As I watched him sleep, I was suddenly overwhelmed with a flood of pleasurable memories that the two of us have shared including a cross-country trip we took together in the very same Cabriolet. I reflected on our childhood family vacations in Sagaponack, traditional Christmas' at our late grandparents' house, and overnight business ventures at the office. We grew very close over the years, especially after both of our parents passed, and even though neither of us would admit it, we truly enjoyed one another's company. We had our share of fights, like all brothers do, but I always believed that anger could be an exaggerated and exhausted substitute for love.

I wondered if the two of us would have been friends if we weren't brothers. I would have liked to think so, being that we shared so many things in common, but how many of our similarities were due to our mutual environmental and familial influences?

Why am I having these thoughts now? I questioned. *Why am I assessing our relationship as if it were coming to a close?*

Rob's mind was racing through memories of his own as he slept beside me. As I watched him toss and turn on the passenger's seat, I surmised he wasn't rehashing the same relaxing thoughts I was. I reluctantly pressed play on my mental VCR and enjoyed the rest of my memorable feel-good reruns.

My reminiscing put me at ease, maybe a little too at ease, because my thoughts swiftly dissolved from my past to the expectation of the hotel pillow caressing my head. It was as if I was there already, under the covers, retiring peacefully for the night.

I closed my eyes.

"Look out!" Rob screamed. He was now awake.

I opened my eyes.

Through the rain-stained windshield, I noticed what Rob was making all the fuss about. The guardrail.

A flash of lightning brightened the angry skies to accentuate the oncoming fence, as if taunting two doomed souls with a clear look at the beholder of their demise.

I was stunned, too frightened to react. Rob grabbed the wheel from the passenger's seat and tried to steer the Cabriolet to safety, but it was too late. I prepared myself as we crashed through the guardrail. My seatbelt pinned me tightly into my seat like the shackles binding a condemned murderer to the electric chair. I waited for the governor to give the 'okay' and the executioner to pull the lever.

I should have worried more about owning a car without an airbag system than complaining about a broken radio, I thought, recognizing the deathtrap that was my car.

The golf clubs in the backseat were singing and dancing for mercy as the car ricocheted down a steep wooded hill. Rob had given up trying to navigate our way through the oaks standing menacingly in our path.

The front right wheel slammed into a rock jutting out of the ground, lifting the car into the air and tossing it over as it smashed into a tree before falling back to earth, upside down.

I should have upgraded to the hard top model.

The car compressed like the bellows of an accordion. Glass and golf clubs were everywhere. I knew I was hurt badly, but luckily and quite astonishingly, I didn't feel any pain. Rob, on the other hand, was suffering. A deep gash on his forehead leaked blood all over his face and shirt.

I hope I don't look like that.

His glazed eyes turned to me as he whispered with all of his energy. "Help me."

I reached over, grabbed his wrist, and held it tightly. "I won't leave you," I said, coughing up blood. I looked down at my stomach. My shirt was bleached red. I felt for a wound. It didn't take long for me to find one. A long deep cut right above my scar from my appendectomy ran across my chest. Strangely still, there was no pain. As I helplessly watched my brother painfully struggle in the last seconds of his life, I naturally questioned the purpose of my short-lived existence.

I should have tasted my cousin's home cooked pasta. I should have been a switch hitter in high school. I should have worked less. I should have been happier, more helpful, more caring. I should have gotten off at that exit.

Aside from my regrets, I was at peace, and I waited patiently for my expiration date. Inauspiciously, my brother's had already expired like a carton of stale milk.

Why was I having an easier time passing than my brother?

◆　　　◆　　　◆

When Rob and I were younger and sharing a bunk bed, we would sometimes stay up all night asking one another how we would want to die. The game was to try to top the other's answer in absurdity and originality. I always came up with the most creative scenarios.

"A bird punctures a hole in my hot air balloon as I attempt the record for fastest solo flight around the world," I explained to my brother, as I planned to outdo his boring alien abduction story. "I spiral uncontrollably down to earth at sonic speeds. As I prepare for a fatal impact, I notice an unidentifiable pile on the rapidly approaching ground, approximately sixty yards from my current location, which seems like it could cushion my fall. I manage to maneuver myself over the mound as I continue to descend, hoping and praying that it is comprised of something soft."

"I thought you were spiraling uncontrollably?" Rob asked.

"I'm the best hot air balloon driver since *The Wizard of Oz,*" I retorted.

Rob playfully poked the bottom of the top bunk, digging his fingers into my mattress and into my back. I hated when he did that, and I was powerless to revenge.

"Anyway," I continued. "I close my eyes and brace for the worst. I think about my *lasts.*

Lasts was another morbid game that Rob and I made up one sleepless night. We would each come up with a series of questions that could not be answered until the last moment of our lives. Questions like, what would be the last movie you ever watch? What would be the last food you ever eat? What would be the last word you ever speak?

The game would be to come up with as many questions like those as we possibly could without ever repeating any, and then remembering them so they could be answered just prior to death. We didn't play Lasts as much as we enjoyed making up the stories behind our demise.

"Gravity takes me right into the unknown pile," I said, as I continued my hot air balloon death story, trying to include as many wild elements as I possibly could in order to win the game. "Luckily, it is soft enough to break my fall and save my life. I take a few moments to regain my composure. However, a foul smell overwhelms my senses. It is an unbearable odor."

My brother had no idea where my story was headed.

"I landed onto a large pile of shit," I continued. "It must be my own, I say to myself. I was so scared while falling, I probably crapped all over the place. I try to escape, but like putrid quicksand, I am pulled into my own mushy excrement. I scream for help, but it is too late. I drown and die."

"You win," Rob reluctantly said, sounding disgusted.

I laughed excitedly. I always won that game. "In all seriousness, what do you think would be the worst way to go?" I asked.

There was a long moment of silence. "Probably to be killed by someone you love," he said.

◆   ◆   ◆

Suddenly, a terrifying realization came over me like a black cloud spewing raindrops of guilt and heartache.

I killed my brother.

With that thought, I felt all of the pain from the car crash surge through my wounds for the first time. I used my last modicum of energy to squeeze Rob's 'pulseless' wrist. "I'm sorry," I whispered.

He couldn't hear me. He couldn't respond.

I let go of my dead brother's wrist and leaned my head against the cold uncomfortable steering wheel, wishing it were a soft pillow at the Marriott Hotel. My head was pressed against the horn, playing the last note of my truncated life. A sardonic sustained B flat.

Without answering any of my lasts, I passed away.

2

HOME AGAIN

Darkness.

"Wake up, honey."

Who was that? A warm familiar hand stroked the top of my head.

"You've been out like a light," the mysterious voice whispered. "We've been waiting for you to join us."

It can't be.

I locked my eyes shut, fighting to keep the tears from escaping.

"Don't be afraid," the female voice said assuredly. "Dinner is almost ready."

She gently kissed me on the forehead. A feeling unfelt since my childhood. Tears swelled under my eyelids and planned their escape. I finally gave in and unlocked the neighboring jail cells. I looked up at …

"Mom!" I cried. She gave me a great big bear hug, another sensation that I sorely longed for. I didn't want to let go. "I missed you so much," I puled over heavy sobs of joy.

Mom momentarily let go of me as she wiped away the tears making their getaway down my face. She looked exactly how I chose to remember her after she died. She appeared young and high-spirited; the mother that did everything for me growing up. She was beautiful. Nothing like the sickly appearance she wore during the last few months of her life as she struggled unavailingly against cancer.

It was always hard for me to visit her at the hospital because I didn't want to remember her in that condition.

And now, I will never have to.

We held each other again ... in eternity.

How fitting. She welcomed me into life, and now ...

I grabbed onto her long silky red hair, never wanting to let go and knowing that I never had to. She smelled of my childhood. An aroma that instantly reminded me of all the after school car rides she provided my friends and me in middle school, and all of the nights I spent sleeping on the floor of her room when Dad was away on business trips so she wouldn't feel alone. Two recollections that I never thought I would nostalgically look back on. *I guess sometimes the mundane are great places to dust for fingerprints when trying to identify the memorable moments in life.*

"There are a lot of people downstairs who want to see you," Mom said. "Take a few minutes and then come down to say hello." She kissed me and walked downstairs.

I was alone to evaluate my situation.

I was in the extension of my grandparents' house. This was an addition to the house where most family holidays and celebrations centered. I was there for the first time since it was refurnished and then demolished some thirty plus years ago. It was exactly how I remembered it. *There isn't a warmer more comforting feeling than to return to a place, which has become dizzy from endlessly cycling the carousel of time, at its most impressionable, most sentient, and most sobering state.*

"Dad was right," I said to myself. "These walls are alive."

I was immediately attracted to the light gray reclining chair in the corner of the dimly lit room. This was my favorite chair growing up.

Situated next to the chair was an antique wooden shoe fitting stool, which was being multi-tasked as an end table. There were a number of cup stains on the stool, like birthday rings on a tree stump, and I wondered how many were left by me.

I jumped on the chair and closed my eyes. I imagined looking out at a sea of Christmas presents piled up to the ceiling fan in the middle of the room. I saw myself as a child climbing up to the peak of the pile as my family assembled around the room armed with cameras. *What a wonderful sight.*

I slowly ran my hand against the grain of the chair's fabric, just like I used to when I slept on it as a child, and the fuzzy sensation on the palm of my hand took me back to places and times too obscure for my memory alone to revive.

It wasn't the most comfortable chair to sleep on, especially when I began to outgrow its recline, but I wouldn't have it any other way.

As I had done a million times before, I lifted the cushion to check for any loose change. I was usually lucky enough to find someone else's pocket scraps deep within the chair's crevice, but years after I thought I had fished through the insides of the chair for the last time, I reeled in something even more special than the usual shiny nickel and the dried out wad of gum.

"Pop-Pop's pipe," I muttered, as I held the item carefully in my hands.

My grandfather's hand carved pipe was just as much a part of him as any of his uniquely identifiable facial features. I hadn't seen him since he died on my eighth birthday, but I never forgot his face. And that pipe.

I wonder if he's downstairs.

I looked over at a picture hanging on the wall just above a bookcase housing old dusty encyclopedias and supporting a stack of hardly viewed National Geographic books. *I remember when Dad and I sold those books at a garage sale.* It was a photo that pictured my father's immediate family, including his mother, father, sister, and three brothers. I hadn't seen that photograph in years.

It's been even longer since the last time I saw any of the people in that photograph.

I was getting excited.

At that moment, all of the sound waves created by my family over the years that these four walls experienced and trapped now passed through my body. They carried me back to the memorable family Christmas traditions discussed and established when I was young enough to believe in Santa Claus.

"Dad was right, again," I told myself. "It's not just the vessel, it's also the space inside that counts." That's what he told me as a bulldozer smashed into the side of the very vessel once built by my grandfather as a gift to his family.

◆   ◆   ◆

Upon hearing about the demise of my father's childhood home, my dad asked me to accompany him to witness a tragic and most solemn day.

According to a bunch of papers, the house was no longer ours, even though the memories would have begged to differ. According to the state of New York, my father's childhood home now belonged to a family from Florida, and their first order of business was to knock down my grandfather's extension to make room for a pool in the backyard.

"It took two years of hard work for your Pop-Pop to build that room," Dad told me. "And it will take two minutes for the construction crew to knock it down."

At eighteen years old, I cried like a baby. I thought to myself, *I'm never going to set foot in the extension ever again.* Memories that were once supported by design and structure now collected in a pile of fallen debris. For the new occupants, it must have been so easy to repave roads without thinking about the stories in every pothole and behind every skid mark. However, at that moment, for my father and me, we could not share their luxury.

"Dad," I said. "All of our memories are in ruins."

I seemed to be more upset than my father was. I wanted to blame the new owners and wondered why we couldn't stop them from destroying our memories. My father calmly put his arm around my shoulders, sensing how upset I was, and said, "It doesn't depend. It isn't the dimensions of the room or the color of the wallpaper. It is the people, the family, and the events that brought those walls to life. Never forget that."

◆   ◆   ◆

"It's not the vessel, it's the space inside that counts," I said to myself, as I traveled through the family photograph hanging on the wall of my grandfather's extension.

I never forgot.

I was ready to say hello.

I dismounted the chair and walked across the room, passing a light green lamp that I remembered accidentally breaking when I was a kid. I had to close my eyes to filter out some of the memories swarming toward me through my heightened senses. There were just too many being evoked by this room for me to handle all at once.

There will be plenty of time for me to experience all of them later.

My nostrils flared as I neared the entranceway. The aromas of familiarity buckled my knees. My perspiring hand gripped onto the black rusted banister as I slowly made my way down the three steps that led into my grandparents' kitchen.

I heard voices. *They're here.*

I entered the kitchen for the first time in over thirty years. Everything had remained the same. The cracked floor tiles, the unemployed dinner bell, the broken clock, the chipped wooden kitchen table, and the unlit light bulb in the ceiling fan; the potholes and skid marks of my grandparents' kitchen.

There he was. My heart skipped a beat. Even with his back turned to me as he washed dishes at the sink, I knew it was him. He looked exactly how I remembered him. Just like in the picture up in the extension.

What should I do? Should I approach him? What if he doesn't remember me? After all, I was only eight years old when he died.

I fished his pipe from my pocket. "Pop-Pop," I choked.

My grandfather didn't seem surprised to hear my voice. He didn't even acknowledge my greeting. Instead, he took his time cleaning the last dish.

Did I do something wrong?

He wiped his hands carefully and methodically with a nearby towel. I could tell that his hands were trembling as he fumbled for the towel.

Did I scare him?

I didn't know what to do.

He finally turned toward me and smiled. A tingling sensation ran up the back of my neck. I had so much to say to him. We had so much to catch up on. "I have your pipe," I said.

A tear streaked down his face as he approached me with open arms. We hugged each other. I wondered if he recognized me as the grown man he never met, or the eight-year-old kid he taught how to swing a golf club.

We didn't speak a word to one another. Not then. Not until we were all together.

I joined Pop-Pop, hand in hand, into the dining room where the rest of the family sat around a long table preparing to eat.

Nobody had to tell me where I was.
I was home.

3

CHRISTMAS EVE

It was Christmas Eve. My favorite time of the year. It was one of the few days that the entire family was able to get together. As time dragged on, the number of leafs comprising our pull-out table reduced so that our holiday dining space could adapt to the unsettling amount of fading family members. But on the day I returned home, Christmas Eve would be celebrated as I remembered it best, which meant the family table would be stretched to its limits for the first time in ages.

"Shush, he's here," Dad joked.

Dad was sitting at the opposite end of the room adjacent to the festively decorated Christmas tree, strumming an acoustic guitar while singing one of his songs.

I haven't heard him in years.

Every night after we'd finish watching the Yankees game, we'd go upstairs where Dad would give me a personal concert. I'd lie on the floor in front of him, listening and singing along. He loved to play the Beatles and Johnny Cash, but he especially enjoyed writing and performing his own music. Some of my fondest memories were in the studio playing drums on his new songs.

Dad sang as I soaked in beautiful memories.

As soon as you realize you notice the light,
Free to be selfish, you've earned the right,
Succumb to the struggle, the turn of the tide,
Fresh out of wisdom, ahead of one's time.

I never completely understood his lyrics.

Everybody was here. It was as if I was watching a movie. But everything was real. I felt the unconditional love from my family as I inched my way further into the room.

Mom, Aunt Carol, and Aunt Anne exchanged envelopes containing the receipts to their respective Christmas shopping purchases. Uncle Kenny and Uncle Michael blindly taste-tested two comparative bottles of red wine and subsequently argued over their subjective findings. Uncle Ricky hovered over a dictionary sniffing loudly while in pursuit of the perfect word for the Dictionary Game.

I'm sure there is no word in there to describe the way I am feeling right now.

Uncle Vinny was finishing the last of his dinner.

Nothing had changed.

"Did you see the amount of gifts in the poolroom?" Uncle Ricky asked.

"The Christmas pile is going to have both height and girth this year," Uncle Kenny commented. "We outdid ourselves again."

My presence seemed to have surprised no one, as if I was here all along. Maybe I was. There was one thing I knew for sure. I never wanted to leave.

"We put the *mas* in Christmas," I said, proving that I was still a seasoned veteran to the whole family Christmas tradition.

Our Christmas traditions have been woven tightly into the family fabric. To the outsider, it may have looked like our traditions hinged on the materialistic, being that our Christmas shopping began in August and that our playful overanalyzing of the size of the Christmas pile on Christmas Eve sometimes made us appear rapacious, but the traditions were always grounded in something much more fundamental than the proverbial 'mas' we put in Christmas. It was predicated on family.

I understood that tradition was not an existential idea or an intangible feeling. It was a place, a place of utmost happiness. It was a joyous abode where the harmony of the mind could manifest. And I was back.

I was a child again. I felt like taking refuge under the table and surreptitiously playing with everybody's shoelaces. I felt like being a contestant in my Uncle Ricky's annual Christmas Eve game. I felt like opening up one of my stocking gifts. I felt like shooting pool downstairs in the billiards room.

However, something wasn't right. I couldn't put my finger on it though. Something was missing and it made the pit in my stomach churn.

As if waiting for her cue, my grandmother walked in carrying a tray of monster meat specifically for me. *The missing link?* She kissed me on the cheek and put the plate of meat on the table. "Your favorite," she told me.

My favorite.

I was referring to my grandmother. She was referring to the meat.

To me, Grandma was the lifeline to the family as a queen bee is to her colony. She was the adhesive that kept everyone together, and preserved many of our unwritten traditions. Whenever I saw her, I felt at home, even when her age was taking its toll. Each wrinkle on her face carried a lifetime of countless stories that I continually tried to read with my lips. Maybe it was just an excuse to kiss her and show my affection for my only grandmother. I was always proud that she never tried to censor her stories with a mask of makeup. Some people have a lot of character in their faces. I hoped that I was one of the many characters that made up my grandmother's. I could always count on her to set the family's heartbeat for all of our get-togethers, and I loved her eternally for that.

"I'm sorry, Grandma," I said.

I was at the hospital when she died. I was seventeen years old. I experienced a dizzying array of emotions ranging from profound sadness and engrossed loneliness to unrefined anger. I was afraid for the future of the family's cohesion and I blamed my grandmother for leaving us forever. *When the queen bee dies, the entire colony collapses.* I feared the same would happen to my family. I was so incensed by her abandonment that I didn't attend her funeral. While I stayed at home and sulked, everybody else paid his or her respects. I was alone. I eventually realized that it wasn't my grandmother who was tearing the family apart. Even at her funeral, she had managed to bring everybody together and I was trying to stop it.

"Eat up," she told me. I pulled the plate of monster meat toward me as I sat down at the table.

Monster meat was nothing more than small chunks of beef, but when I was a child, I imagined they held some sort of magical power that gave me the uncanny ability to destroy monsters. Not that I tended to have an inordinate number of run-ins with potent creatures at my grandmother's house.

It was always better to play it safe.

I would scarf down three servings of monster meat and be ready for battle. Sometimes, I would even make believe that Rob was a monster, and I would attack him, only to be reprimanded by my grandmother for ruthlessly picking an unfair fight.

I couldn't eat. I was grateful for my grandmother's cooking, but my stomach didn't feel right. Unbelievably, something was still missing.

How selfish could I be?

"Rob!" I shouted, discovering the missing link. "Where's Rob?"

Even though I had not seen Grandma until her warm welcome in the dining room, I felt her presence from the moment I opened my eyes in the extension. I knew she was there all along. Just as I knew Pop-Pop would be waiting for me in the kitchen. Therefore, it wasn't her temporary absence that was feeding my sudden stomach pains. It was my brother's.

Where could he be?

It was then that I noticed the vacant spot at the table where Rob used to sit. Something told me that he wouldn't be joining us. I couldn't hone in on his vibe or pick up on his scent anywhere.

"Where's Rob?" I asked again.

There was a moment of awkward silence that was doing an odd number on my stomach. My first uncomfortable sensation since I had come back.

Grandma nervously cleared her throat as she sat down at the table. Dad stopped singing and rested the guitar on his lap. Pop-Pop lit his pipe and quietly stared longingly at the falling snow through the dining room window. Uncle Ricky closed the dictionary and played eye tag with the rest of the hesitant family.

Why isn't anybody saying anything?

"Has anybody seen Rob?" I asked again nervously. Maybe he was down in the poolroom chalking the pool cues and racking the balls in preparation for one of our bloody competitions. "What's going on?"

"I think I saw him hanging around the shed," Pop-Pop muttered in a borderline whisper of nervous incoherence. "He went in."

"The shed!" I shrieked. *Not the shed.*

A sharp pain tore uncharitably through my lower abdomen.

Mom sat beside me and rubbed my back as I bent over in pain. "Don't get yourself all worked up about Rob," Mom told me, as the rest of the family nodded in agreement. "You've made it. You're here with all of us."

"What do you mean?" I asked. "He's not going to be with us?"

"He didn't make it," Uncle Ricky said while fighting back an emotion.

He didn't make it?

I mentally replayed the car crash and saw the big gash in Rob's head collecting small chunks of windshield as he hunched over to take in his final breath.

He was definitely killed in the crash, I thought, trying to figure out where he might have gone. *The shed. Why would he ever enter the very place that had once provided us with a lifetime of horrific nightmares?*

"You are very fortunate," Uncle Michael said while sipping his wine. "In the final hour, Rob had been judged unfairly, and there is nothing we can do about it."

It suddenly made perfect sense. Uncle Ricky was right. Rob didn't make it.

The jury had reached a more severe verdict in his case. He was unjustly condemned to a place that was the complete antithesis of my light sentence to eternal euphoria. And if we truly received diametric verdicts, which still didn't make much sense why, then based solely upon how wondrous of a place I was in, I concluded that he must undoubtedly be in hell.

Hell. The thought of thinking about the word made me tremble. That was what he called the shed when we were growing up.

"Why don't we bring the Christmas presents up now," Dad said awkwardly, trying to change our topic of conversation to something more pleasant.

I was too distressed to feel at home any longer. The roof to my joyous abode had come crashing down like the Hindenburg over a Jersey field, and all of the pain from my fatal car crash had once again swelled through my insides. I knew that whatever hurt I was feeling was no match to the misery that Rob was being subjected to. The thought of my brother suffering alone conjured up disturbing images of his experiences in our grandparents' shed. Tremendous guilt displaced my euphoria.

I'm the one in hell, I assessed.

I hogged all of the overwhelmingly enjoyable memories during our final car ride while Rob slept through a nightmare on the passenger's seat. I was then bombarded with a lifetime of more unforgettable moments while reconvening with my family in the very home where our traditions prospered, as Rob continued to flee from his nightmares, by himself, in the ultimate evil.

It wasn't fair. And I felt guilty.

I killed him. The thought once again made me shudder. *I sent him to hell. If I had just gotten off at that exit, then he would still be alive and we would still be together.*

Everyone got up from the table, leaving me to my thoughts, and made their way through the kitchen and toward the large mass of Christmas presents scattered throughout the poolroom. The whole scene was a blur to me as I continued to sit motionless, in shock, calculating Rob's misfortunate situation against my utopia.

"Why didn't he make it? Surely, it was a mistake!" I yelled.

"It is what it is," Aunt Carol responded. "Nothing can be done."

"We're all here for you," Aunt Anne commented. "You deserve your slice of heaven. Precisely how you always envisioned your perfect recipe would be."

How could my so-called perfect cake not include my brother? I wondered.

"Come on," Dad shouted, attempting to distract me from my concern over Rob. "We need an extra person for our human chain."

"We really topped ourselves this year," Uncle Kenny remarked, also trying to take my mind off my thoughts.

Normally, I would have jumped at the occasion to help bring the gifts up to the extension. It was my first opportunity of the season at accurately estimating how many presents in the pile were for me. Sometimes I'd even peek through the wrapping paper and ruin my Christmas surprise. Rob and I liked to guess what each gift was as we handed them off to the next person in the human chain. It was easy to recognize the hockey sticks and the baseball bats. Any normal sized rectangular box was always some sort of clothing item. Weight was always factored into our guesses.

It was most exciting to be assigned to the beginning of the chain, in the poolroom, because then it was a complete surprise to see how the end of the chain managed piling the presents around the room. *Did they go for height this year or girth?* It was also interesting to hear the comments about the pile filtered down from the top of the chain like a child's game of telephone. "Christmas didn't come this year," Uncle Ricky would joke. It never got old, especially the subsequent hours of sitting around the pile telling stories while anticipating new ones. However, none of those memories mattered anymore.

"Are you coming?" Dad shouted, as I continued to process my heavy thoughts at the dining room table, alone and in silence.

"All of the gifts are for you again this year," Uncle Vinny interjected.

How could they not do anything about Rob?

I got up and slowly made my way to the kitchen window. I peered over at the shed. Everything I presumed about Rob's whereabouts was now confirmed. The sight of it demanded my attention, and for Rob's sake, I couldn't look away.

Rob is lost somewhere in there.

"We vowed never to set foot in there again," I grumbled to myself.

All that I had experienced on the other side of life, up until I gazed through the kitchen window and into the wintry night, had appeared exactly how I remembered them best, including my family. My grandmother's shed, however, flaunted all of time's undesired side effects, and loomed both haunting and unwelcoming. The glass window was cracked, the wood facing was rotted out, and the front door flapped open and shut in the breeze as if waving for more visitors to scrutinize the darkened, rat-infested interior.

The scars and pimples of time.

The menacing shed was in direct contrast to what I was experiencing, and what I imagined I would find in there would be nothing like any Christmas Eve past.

The shed door swung open, daring me to find out. "I've got to help Rob," I concluded.

4

MONGO AND THE CLOWN

It seemed to grow out of the center of the carpet and spread across the room like a disease. They went for girth. As if like a campfire, it called the family to gather around to reminisce, share, and continue the family's most sacred tradition.

It was just as I remembered.

"I see carpet," Dad joked. "Christmas didn't come this year."

"On a scale of one to ten," Uncle Ricky inquired, "how does this Christmas rate compared to all of our others?"

This would normally be the time when Rob and I would argue over who would be the first to wake up on Christmas morning, which would then escalate into an even more heated argument about who was always the one to wake up the earliest on the holiest of holy days. This debate never got old and we seldom reached an agreement. Any semblance of naming a winner got lost in semantics. We had different interpretations of the definition of 'waking up.' Rob believed that it counted if you opened your eyes up for a moment and then fell back asleep, whereas I believed you must have every intention of staying up for the day in order to be crowned the champion.

I smiled.

After all of these years, the family didn't miss a beat.

"Tomorrow, when we open up the presents," my Dad expressed jokingly, establishing the next morning's ground rules, "no trying on any clothes or assembling any electronics until everybody has opened up all of their gifts."

Everybody nodded and then erupted into an excited giggle, knowing that all of the ground rules would be broken.

Even though I had front row seats with backstage access to heaven, I sat in silence and wondered why no one in the family was concerned about Rob. *Why was everyone able to laugh so easily and accept Rob's absence? Surely, they couldn't feel that the family was complete without him.*

As I continued to watch the family bask in eternal joy, I couldn't take it anymore. I was about to ruin everybody's joyous holiday. "I'm going to get Rob," I preached, silencing my family.

The conflagration in the fireplace took advantage of the room's silence to tauntingly snap at me with its red-hot arms.

"That's impossible," Dad said.

"Where are you going to go?" Mom asked uneasily.

"I'm going to start where you saw him last," I said. "In the shed."

The family, still silent, looked toward each other for someone to respond.

"If you leave," Dad continued, "you'll never be able to come back." He tried to sound as authoritative as a dad could be to make me feel like the child I longed to remember. "Don't you think we're all upset about your brother's destiny?" Dad responded. "If there was something we could do, we would do it. You'll be damned for all eternity if you enter that shed." He quieted momentarily, a dramatic pause, and looked directly into my eyes, searching for a nerve to strike with his hammer of guilt. "And then, I'll have two doomed sons lost forever."

I was disappointed that Dad was not supportive of my decision to go after my brother, his son, since he was the one who first taught me the meaning and importance of preserving family. I never felt so alone, and I wasn't bluffing. The silence in the room was deafening except for the snapping flames.

Dad again looked at me straight in the eyes and sighed. "Nobody comes back."

I studied the faces of my family, and for the first time, I couldn't feel a connection to any of them.

"It's a one-way ticket," Uncle Ricky interjected.

Dad shifted nervously in his seat, and everybody got up at once, almost as if all of their mental alarms were set for the same exact time. I remained seated.

"It is getting late," Grandma said while yawning. "We'll have a wonderful Christmas and then we can talk more about this situation after you've had time to adjust."

There it was. I only caught a glimpse of it through the space between the gifts in the Christmas pile, but it was definitely there. I was getting a positive read on my grandma's face. She was giving me tacit approval to my journey.

"It's bedtime," Uncle Michael exhaled.

I could use a good night's sleep. The last time I thought about sleep was just before my fatal car accident. *My lasts.* I promised myself to try to get a good night's sleep and to be prepared, but not knowing what for. Everyone gave me a kiss on the cheek before retiring for the night. Their last push at keeping me right where I belonged. I was once again alone in the extension.

My loneliness made me very sleepy. My thoughts were overly consumed with questions concerning the reasons as to why Rob didn't make the party. *Maybe his invitation got lost in the mail.*

I had only one thing to do. I was going to personally hand deliver his invitation to him, and, against all odds, chauffeur him back.

I fell asleep on the reclining gray chair, and for the first time in years, I experienced my recurring childhood nightmare. Inauspiciously, this version happened to be more lucid than I had ever imagined.

◆　　　◆　　　◆

A light drizzle doused the twilight sky as I held onto my parents' arms and swung back and forth in-between my two makers with my six-year-old legs off the ground. We were searching for our car in the circus parking lot.

"We parked in section F-25," Mom guessed unsurely.

"No, it was next to the blue jeep," Dad joked.

As we continued to walk aimlessly through the sea of cars, my attention was abruptly diverted toward a nearby circus clown. He was filling his car's open trunk to the brim with colorful balloons. I gripped my parents' hands tighter as we neared him.

"Did you like the circus?" Mom asked me.

"I liked the rings of fire," I said nervously, hoping I wouldn't be noticed by the clown. My fight or flight response had been activated. The clown had his back to me and luckily did not sense my presence or smell my squalid odor of fear.

Hurry up and find the car, I prayed. *Get me outta here.*

Dad pulled out the map as he and my mom stopped right in front of the clown to locate our bearings. At that moment, I hated my parents. Even though they were most likely clueless to my apprehensiveness, I blamed them for purposely tormenting me in the white face of my greatest phobia. I tried to play it cool, hoping not to make an embarrassing scene. The sweat from my palms loosened my grip on my parents' arms. There was no place I could hide from the clown. I knew it was only a matter of time before he would turn around and see me.

"You see, here's the entrance," Dad explained, as he pointed to the map. "We parked in lot A … I think. Where's lot A?"

I wanted to scream for them to hurry up. The clown's trunk was almost congested with balloons. *He's going to turn soon.*

"He looks like he works here," Mom said, pointing to the clown. "Let's ask him."

"No," I whispered, which sounded more like a scream in my head.

I tried hiding behind my mom's legs, but it was too late. He noticed us. The clown wore a wig of curly rainbow hair. His red plastic nose and his painted red mouth accentuated his heavenly white face to hide the darkness of evil under his skin.

He spotted me and smiled.

"Parking lot A is across the street," he offered, directing us with his oversized glove. Even though the clown was talking to my parents, he didn't take his eyes off me. His unvarying smirk and his unblinking eyes buckled my knees like a batter expecting a fastball, but getting a slow curve.

"Would you like a balloon?" he asked, as he waved for me to draw nearer to him. I shivered, my eyes beginning to water. And still, my parents didn't recognize any of my symptoms. "Pick out a balloon. They come in all colors." The clown laughed haughtily from deep within his gut.

"Don't be afraid," Dad said. "Take a balloon for the ride home."

The clown's smile grew. "Come with me," he said.

I didn't move, but my mind was racing.

"I know what you did," the clown told me, his voice turning stern.

I know what you did. I replayed the clown's comment in my head. *What did I do? How would he know anything I did anyway?* The clown started approaching me. I wanted to dig myself into the ground and hide away forever.

"You killed your brother," the clown sneered, as he inched his way closer and closer toward me. "You drove him right into a tree and bashed his fucking brains in." I was within his grasp.

I couldn't hold it in any longer. Just as the tears poured out from my cloudy eyes, the skies opened up and cried.

"Don't feel bad," the clown said. His makeup was being washed away by the steady rainfall to unveil the grim face of death, the root of all evil, the seed of all fear. "A balloon will lift your spirits."

I screamed aloud, which sounded more like a whisper in my head. The balloons in the clown's trunk floated up into the angry sky. There must have been hundreds of them flying high above us. The clown laughed. "Would you like to come for a ride?" Death asked.

I looked at the car, which now resembled a black hearse. Something was moving in the backseat. At a closer glance, I noticed who it was. I gasped. It was Rob. He was tied up in the backseat, his mouth gagged, as he stared back longingly for help.

"Rob!" I screamed. "Where are you taking him?"

My brother turned, exposing the bloody gash in the back of his head, and then vanished into the darkness of the car's interior. The grim reaper laughed a circus clown's laugh.

I looked up at my parents for support. Instead, I almost lost my balance and fainted. They both wore clown costumes. I screamed again, and this time loud enough for my brain to appreciate the decibels. I tried to let go of them, but they held onto my hands tightly, and not even my sweat could loosen their grip. Mom and Dad joined in with bellows of laughter as they dragged me toward the smiling clown who now stood by my grandparents' open shed door, waving for me to enter.

"Let me go!" I screamed. The friction that my shoes engendered with the parking lot blacktop did very little at holding me back. I looked up into the sky and prayed to become one of the balloons soaring toward the heavens.

In a last-ditch effort, I shrieked, "I want to go home!"

◆   ◆   ◆

Grandma leaned over me and felt my forehead. "You're burning up," she told me.

I glanced over at the blinking time on the VCR. It read 3:30 A.M.

I've been asleep for two hours. I was the first one up on Christmas morning. *If only Rob were here.*

Grandma looked around the dark extension before touching her warm lips to my responsive ear.

I was still recovering from my nightmare, but my grandmother's presence seemed to be the perfect ointment for my formidable mental ailment.

"Everybody's asleep," she whispered. "I've packed you a bag of monster meat for the trip," she added.

I immediately perked up.

She handed me my brother's first grade Power Ranger's knapsack. It was Rob's favorite book bag growing up. He thought he was invincible whenever he put it on. He hoped it would repel the many bullies who agitated him during recess.

◆   ◆   ◆

Never the one to assign supernatural powers to an inanimate object such as a knapsack, I constantly berated my brother with playful verbal jests for his naivety to reverence.

"Don't be a fool," I'd tell him. "How can a canvas pouch strapped to your back make you stronger?"

He continued wearing it though, up through fifth grade, and it was attached to him the day he beat up the meanest, most dreaded bully in the entire school. His performance was the talk amongst his classmates, and it convinced me that his Power Ranger book bag might have played a small unearthly role in his underdog thrashing.

I was a believer.

Mongo had been taking Rob's lunch money all year. His entire week's allowance went right to the self-serving pilfer. Rob would also come home from school every day, clearly upset, and cry through double homework sessions.

I knew what was troubling him, but I promised not to tell our parents.

Halloween was his final straw. Rob and I had dressed up as ghosts that year. We made out pretty well with our stash of candy after circling our neighborhood a few dozen times. Rob stored his winnings in his favorite Power Ranger knapsack. I kept mine in a black garbage bag. Like everything we did together, we made trick-or-treating a competition. Whoever collected more candy was crowned the Halloween champion.

I was probably the only kid who didn't like candy, but the competitor in me did everything possible to outstrip Rob's annual gritty candy collecting performance.

We finished our last lap around the neighborhood searching for any houses with bowls of candy on their front stoop, usually left there by people in a last-ditch effort to get rid of the rest of their treats before the holiday's end.

"My bag weighs more than yours," I taunted.

"I have more candy in my bag," Rob retorted. "We'll count when we get home."

Just then, Mongo, wearing a devil's costume, turned the corner and accidentally bumped into Rob's shoulder, knocking him down, and spilling his candy all over the sidewalk. Mongo was momentarily taken aback. He appeared agitated that somebody would have the audacity to crash into him.

Rob was shaken on the ground from the potency of their impact, hoping that he wouldn't be noticed underneath his costume.

"I'm so sorry," Rob muttered through the sweltering rubber ghost mask.

Mongo laughed and approached my helpless brother.

"Do you know who I am?" Mongo asked.

I couldn't believe how big he was. *The legend was true.* He was three years younger than me, but twice as tall, and I couldn't imagine how much stronger. He stood directly over my brother like a lawless surgeon over an unsuspecting patient. His red horns glimmered underneath the bright street lamp.

If only Rob were a real ghost, he could disappear into the night unharmed.

Mongo revealed the whimpering boy behind the mask with one swipe of his size thirteen boot. It was Mongo's lucky day. Another Halloween surprise.

"Well, if it isn't Casper the nerdy ghost," Mongo sneered.

"Leave me alone," Rob cried. "I'll give you twice the amount of money for lunch tomorrow if you let us go."

"Are you trying to bribe me?" Mongo replied, as he stepped gently on Rob's hand and slowly applied pressure. Rob winced in pain, too proud to surrender to hysteria.

I didn't know what to do. Like the incident on the golf course, I remained idle, leaving my brother once again to fend for himself.

I was getting good at playing the silent partner.

"Oh, don't worry," Mongo said. "I *will* take your money. But first, I think I'll have your candy." Mongo, with his foot still squeezing the blood from Rob's white hand, collected all of Rob's candy strewn haphazardly on the sidewalk and stashed them in his pillowcase. Rob was horrified. All of the effort he put into assembling a noticeable candy score that Halloween was in vain, and all I could think about was whether this meant that I won this year's competition or if it was now considered a draw by default.

Rob clutched onto the shoulder strap of his book bag as he watched Mongo steal everything that he worked for that day. I could tell in my brother's eyes that he wasn't going to give up his candy so easily.

"No," I whispered to him.

He was going to do the unthinkable.

"You're going to get yourself killed," I warned.

His mind was made up. I saw his decision gush from his determined eyes. He was going to stand up to this bully in the devil costume, and stop his trepidation once and for all.

He's committing suicide.

The next thing that happened has since been talked about for years. The story, which has taken on a life of its own, continues to be passed down in the schoolyard from generation to generation. And along the way, this fantastic David and Goliath story has evolved into a classic folklore tale. Some of the versions that I've heard included otherworldly appearances and mystical powers. One story even involved shoelaces, a pair of scissors, and a UFO.

However, I was there to see the beating firsthand. I knew what really happened.

As the palm of my brother's hand began to bleed under Mongo's muddy shoe, Rob swung his book bag around as a railroad steel driver wheels his hammer, and smashed it into the back of Mongo's stunned head. The bully staggered backward, momentarily releasing Rob's pinned hand long enough for him to free himself. Rob quickly affixed the bag on his back and lunged for Mongo. As he leaped onto his opponent and tackled him to the ground, I could have sworn I saw his Power Ranger book bag emanate a radiant golden halo and fuse into his body.

A small crowd of trick-or-treaters hurried from all directions to watch my brother pound in Mongo's face until it matched the color of his bloody hand. He sat on Mongo's chest screaming and crying while continuously hammering away at his nose with both fists. Every time Rob would wind up for his next punch, some of his candy would spill out of his backpack, but the energy it diffused into my brother's muscles amplified exponentially with each passing blow.

"He's killing him!" an excited Jack-in-the-Box screamed.

"Is that … Mongo?" an oversized pumpkin asked.

Nobody, including me, could understand how it happened.

The one-sided affair lasted no more than a few minutes before it was ultimately broken up. However, the damage was done. The giant had been taken down to size.

The two fighters were pulled to opposite sides of the human ring. Mongo, too embarrassed to face his audience, cried as he cowardly scampered into the woods.

Rob instantly became a hero at school, and predictably, was never picked on by Mongo ever again. I later asked Rob, who was now brimming with confidence, what empowered him to do what most people thought was unthinkable.

"I wasn't alone out there," he told me. "Something during the fight had my back."

He winked at me and reached for his favorite Power Ranger knapsack, which he now wore every day. *Something had his back*. I knew exactly what he was talking about because I saw the magic it commissioned firsthand.

I enjoyed listening to others tell the story of the night my brother beat up the biggest, meanest, and dirtiest bully that ever passed through the school system, even though most of the best storytellers were never witness to it. I could have corrected the innumerable erroneously borderline science fiction stories that projected Rob as a godly figure, but I didn't want to shatter everyone's faith.

Sometimes it's better to print the legend instead of the truth because the legend may carry more weight and span longer distances in time.

Looking back, I couldn't ascertain for sure whether the magic that eluded from Rob's book bag was either the glow from the street lamp playing tricks on my imagination or a truly divine experience.

I chose to believe the latter. The legend. So did my brother who was on a desperate quest for something to believe in, whether it was an omnipotent force or the space within himself.

Rob had finally found faith in his book bag, and much like how Catholics display their creed in gold jewelry crosses, my brother donned his icon to spread the gospel of his religion to any apostle willing to follow.

It doesn't matter if the powers these icons exude really provide a spiritual uplifting from an existential being or not. As long as they afford the believer with a small degree of self-confidence and a feeling of inner worth, the magic they summon is real. Anything less or more would be blasphemous.

◆　　　◆　　　◆

"You should leave before they wake up," Grandma said. "Maybe you will find your way back in time to open up your Christmas gifts."

I didn't know what to say. Grandma was letting me go. This was the best Christmas gift she could possibly give me.

I saw the concern in her eyes. She knew that I was about to embark on a very dangerous road. A one-way road that modern lore has defined as hardly traversed and never defeated. But the concern in Grandma's eyes was compounded with confidence. I understood my purpose in them. There was no turning back now.

She hugged me. "Bring him home safely," she urged.

"I will," I promised. "I love you."

I took my brother's book bag, which my grandmother packed with monster meat, and exited Pop-Pop's extension for the last time.

I won't forget the space between these four walls this time around, I thought while holding Grandma's hand. We descended the steps together en route to the dormant kitchen.

I was immediately attracted to the window.

I strained to study the shed, my new destination, but it was too dark outside to see, and I was too tired to process any semblance of a meaningful rumination, but it was there. I sensed its presence circulating through my veins and arteries affecting the cadence of my heart.

I was somewhat relieved that I couldn't distinguish the shed or hear its counterfeit swan call. I didn't need to be reminded of anything that might be giving me any second thoughts.

Except, that is, for the rest of my family.

I owed it to them to say my goodbyes, even if they didn't support my decision.

I never knew if I was ever going to see them again.

I kissed everyone on the cheek and wished them Merry Christmas.

I felt like I had been lost at sea for thirty years, and after finally being rescued and brought back home, I willingly jumped back into the murky shark-infested waters to once again leave everything comfortable behind.

I came to Dad's room. I left the hardest one for last.

I approached his bedside as a survivor nears a loved one's coffin. As I focused on my father's motionless face as he slept silently in bed, it reminded me of the last time I was saying my final farewell to his sickly appearance, which was poorly concealed by a thick layer of unprofessionally applied makeup at the funeral home. It took me a very long time to pay my respects that day in front of my father's empty vessel.

It's not the vessel, I remembered my father lecturing me. *It's the space inside that counts.*

But what occupies the space of a lifeless body? If the soul really rises from the insignificant tangible remains of a human being, then the priceless space inside a body that bestows meaning to its existence in life has jumped ship in death, and has fled as far away from its physical counterpart as possible.

I didn't know a life without Dad until I turned my back on him when the funeral home janitor told me I had to leave his side because it was closing time. I understood that deifying the body in death was both unfair and inappropriate. I had to find the space within, which had once uniquely identified my father, in order to truly honor and revive his energy. I knew it would be a lifelong investigation, which probably wouldn't end until I was lucky enough to depart from my own vessel.

Here we were. Both of our energies were together again in the same space.

My investigation was finally over.

And just as our respective energies had irrevocably fused into one vibrant force (with our opportunely evacuated vessels decaying in airtight solitary jars six feet under the ground), I would have to learn once again to adapt to a life without my father.

I was destined for another investigation. The space within my brother's vessel had been accidentally trapped inside his buried coffin so that nobody could ever recall his spirit or exalt his intangible expanse again. It was my job to set him free so that the family's energy could glow even brighter than before.

"Goodbye, Dad," I cried, as I kissed his cheek.

"You should go before it gets too late," Grandma whispered, as she crept up from behind me. Grandma took my hand, and just like the funeral home's late night janitor, she led me away from my resting Dad … for good … again.

Was I making the right decision?

Seeing everybody for the last time really waived my decisiveness through the third base coach's stop sign. Nobody was going to stand in my way.

I needed to add the last plank, the final building block, in order to slide safely into the perfect home for the final run in extra innings … sudden death.

Who am I? What makes me think that I am the only one who feels obligated to save my brother, and confident that it can be done?

"It's a one-way ticket," I remember Uncle Ricky foreboding.

"I'm scared," I said to myself, as Grandma walked me to the front door. I was always afraid of change, which was why my comforting memories were so important to my mental health, and after living the ultimate memory in death, I was forced to undertake the biggest change of my existence; a frighteningly unsettling prospect.

That's hell. For me, at least.

There was one more person left to hear my goodbyes. I turned to my grandmother and weighed her eyes to see if she lost any of the confidence she carried in her boundless and timeless pupils. She hadn't. Her eyes urged me on.

"Come here," she said with her arms open.

To me, this was her second funeral and just like her first one, there was a good chance that I was never going to see her again. But for this service, I needed to be with her to pay my respects and say goodbye.

I wasn't going to make the same mistake twice.

"Why are you letting me go?" I had to know.

"I am not going to make the same mistake twice," she responded. "This time, I won't be so naive."

I hugged her and kissed her cheek gently, refusing to expose my agitation, and hoping for one last word of wisdom. I read the story on her face with my quivering chapped lips as a blind man's fingers graze the freckles of his literature. It read, with confidence, "If you seek out your destiny and search for your heart's desire, then you will forever be home."

It was time. We let go of one another.

"Be safe," Grandma pleaded.

Armed only with monster meat, I took one last look at a version of my past that I feared I would never be able to recapture.

5

MAKING THE LEAP

The air was thick with humidity, making it hard to breathe. Not the kind of environment you'd expect to have on Christmas morning on Long Island. Or was the dense air possibly replete with an excess of heavy memories waiting to precipitate?

The heat was so intense; I was frozen in my tracks. With each step down my grandparents' stoop, I forged into the oven of time, sweating every memory from my soul onto my shirt.

The distinct aroma of freshly cut grass, chlorine, and propane made no doubt that it was summertime. Each droplet of sweat contained a memory complete in its own DNA. From stoopball to collecting cicada bugs, to waiting impatiently for Mr. Softee, I was transported to a time where innocence was a right not having to be proved. I was seven years old.

I placed my hand on the rusted railing to regain my reality, but instead, I felt myself brush against another memory as I pulled at the thorns of an adjacent bush.

◆   ◆   ◆

"What are you so scared of?" Uncle Ricky would tease. "Don't be a baby. Stand on the railing and jump over the bush."

Uncle Ricky would pressure me to balance myself on the three-inch wide railing, like a gymnast poised on a balance beam, and encourage me to perform a five foot high dismount over the bush and onto the lawn.

"Get up there!" Uncle Ricky would bark impatiently.

During most of my lessons, I would cowardly walk away from the obstacle only to be berated by my uncle for "being a weenie."

Eventually, I would get to the top of the railing, but I would still be too frightened to stand completely upright, and would rather partake in the forced march of shame in front of my uncle than to make the leap over the bush.

I also hated when Uncle Ricky would bring up my failure at the dinner table in front of the whole family. He was overtly taunting me, and everyone else would join in with unruly fits of laughter.

"He can't even jump over a little bush," he would tell everyone. "How do you expect him to accomplish anything in life if he can't do something so simple?"

I was only a little kid and those comments really disturbed me. I knew Uncle Ricky was just saying those things to inspire me. There was only one way to put an end to the nasty derisions. I was determined to conquer my fears and prove to my uncle, and most importantly to myself, that I was capable of jumping over that bush.

It was the Fourth of July, and following our traditional barbeque at my grandparents' house, we were going to Jones Beach to view the fireworks. Once I discovered that Uncle Ricky would be at Grandma's, I began preparing for my moment. During the entire car ride, I visualized my jump, clearing the vexatious bush with ease to the tune of a wild and crazy crowd.

I was quiet throughout the entire trip and my parents suspected that something was up. "Cat got your tongue?" Mom asked.

I didn't say a word. I was locked in, completely focused on my goal.

Dad pulled all the way into my grandparents' driveway, right up to the menacing bush so that it fit directly into the frame of my car door window. The bush's razor sharp claws rubbed against the glass. I had no intention of hiding behind my shield forever. I was going to jump as I had never jumped before.

The family greeted us on the front patio, but I bypassed all of them and went straight for the courting bush with its inauspicious fangs.

I stood right on the railing and pushed myself up to the top. The gallery was silent. I heard Aunt Carol hush a laugh and Uncle Ricky exhale in anticipation and uncertainty. Their lack of faith or confidence in me would not stray me off my course.

The balls of my feet searched for a balance as they rocked back and forth along the thin metal tightrope above the ground. I spread my arms out for balance. It was the first time I stood completely erect for over ten seconds on the railing's surface. I peered over the bush and believed I could see the top of the world. Any jitters I had prior to climbing the railing had converted into confidence.

"Easy does it," Uncle Ricky coached, the excitement undulating through each one of his words of wisdom. "Bend your knees slowly and push off."

My once sarcastic audience mutated into a vocal support group as I carefully followed Uncle Ricky's instructions. I bent at the knees and swung my arms back, while continuously adjusting my feet for balance. There was no turning back now.

"You can do it," I heard someone say. I turned off my peripheral sensory receptors so I couldn't distinguish which relative was cheering me on.

In one fluid motion, I sprung back up like an uncompressed slinky and pushed off the railing. I became airborne. I had an aerial view of the bush, and I could have sworn I saw it cowering below my feet. I was finally above it. Not even gravity could bring me down from this high.

I didn't have too much time to admire the view, because soon after, I landed harmlessly on the grass.

My family went crazy. Uncle Ricky was so proud of me. They all rushed over to the lawn and congratulated me for my accomplishment.

They were my Fourth of July fireworks.

Uncle Ricky was right. There was nothing to be scared of after all.

As everyone hugged me, all I could think about was how I was going to jump higher and further on my next try. The rest of the day, and into the years ahead, I would vault the same bush for hours at a time.

Uncle Ricky would monitor every trial with pride.

Jumping that bush was the first serious hurdle that I overcame, and Uncle Ricky hoped it would motivate me into conquering bigger, more momentous barricades in the future with the same conviction and work ethic that he instilled into me at my most permeable age.

Little did I know that it would be the first of many hurdles standing in my way during the indelible human race.

After high school, Uncle Ricky wanted me to graduate from climbing the five foot high railing on my grandparents' front yard to hiking the 20,000 foot high Himalayas in India, a considerably taller hurdle to master. Regardless of my uncle's incessant prodding, I never had the opportunity to make that leap.

"Most of the times, you do not create your own hurdles," Uncle Ricky would tell me. "But you must be primed for every scenario and attack them with just as much vigor as the ones that you originate yourself. That's the definition of survival. That's how you win the race."

◆   ◆   ◆

I closed my eyes and continued to run my hands along the bush's prickly epidermis. I didn't know how long it had been since I left my grandmother in the doorway because I was too busy playing leapfrog with the bush and landing back in time to revisit my pioneer hurdle.

It felt like an eternity though.

The sound of a bee buzzing around my head seized my attention.

I opened my eyes. *Where am I?* I thought.

My hand was still stroking a proximate bush, but it wasn't my grandmother's anymore because I was no longer standing in her front yard.

It must be a different bush.

Somehow, I had emerged in front of my childhood home. I slowly spun myself around to digest everything, from my rudimentary tree house in the front yard's Sycamore and the chalk drawings of hopscotch and box ball games on my driveway, to the red door on my celestial white house.

Maybe this is where my brother is, I wished.

The entire neighborhood appeared as I remembered it best.

Another bee flew out from the nearby bush and circled my head.

I caught myself pulling at the bush's inclusive needles, which grew from underneath my mailbox. A bush that my neighbors and I accidentally blew up when I was in sixth grade; a sonic boom.

We called it the burning bush.

◆   ◆   ◆

We were playing wiffle ball in the street, and my friend, Jeff, hit the ball straight into the bee-infested bush, wedging it deep within the contorted branches of the interior, suffocating the plastic ball with a mighty stranglehold of thorns and poison ivy.

Our only wiffle ball was gone. Our game was over.

"Good going, Jeff," I said sarcastically. "How are we going to play now?"

Jeff dangerously reached into the bush with his non-pitching hand and blindly groped for the ball while waving away a hoard of bees from his face with his opposite hand. Jeff's younger brother, Mike, and I watched on with restrained optimism as Jeff extended his arm deeper into the black hole.

There must have been dozens of lost balls in there from over the years. Jeff's chances of locating our wiffle ball were extremely slim.

It was the bees' ball now.

Despite the odds, Mike and I still had hope.

"What goes into the black hole is never lucky enough to find its way back out," we would joke. Tennis balls, baseballs, street hockey balls, all lost their way inside that bush, and most of the times, we never bothered to rescue them.

"Forget it, Jeff," I said, giving up. "We'll never find the ball."

Jeff was determined to beat the bush. "I'm almost there," he said, as he reached in a little bit more. I would have never traveled as far into the bush as Jeff did for something as insignificant as a wiffle ball, especially with a swarm of confused and curious yellow jackets patrolling the area.

Imagine what he would have done if he lost something that truly had meaning in his life, like a brother. Would he have crawled all the way into the bush for the rescue? Would he have taken action and combatted the queen bee with everything he had?

"I got it!" Jeff exclaimed.

Just as he was pulling his arm out to safety, Jeff's face turned white and he let out a high-pitched scream. "I'm stung," he cried out. He backed away from the bush and held his arm out in pain as tears jumped from his eyes. There was no wiffle ball in his hand. The bees had reclaimed it.

There must have been at least ten bite marks on his tender left forearm, and he was feeling the agony swell up from each tiny wound like boiling hot magma out of a chain of active volcanoes. Mike and I couldn't stop giggling as we watched Jeff hold his arm and spin around in circles.

"I'm stung, I'm stung!" he kept yelling out.

"I'll get my dad," I said, as I ran toward my house.

Bags of ice were wrapped tightly around Jeff's arm to stop the swelling. He calmed down, but was still in obvious pain. He joined Mike and me as we watched my dad soak the bush with five cans of Raid.

"They aren't dying," Dad told us.

"So we can't get our ball back?" I asked dejectedly. "Way to go, Jeff."

Dad threw down another empty can of bug poison. "I think these little guys are hornets," Dad said. "The marks on your arm don't look like bee stings." Dad studied the directions on the next full can before shaking it thoroughly. "I don't think these are for hornets. We may need something more powerful."

Jeff stepped up, waving away several stray bees with his good arm. "I have a whole box of M-80's in my garage," he said.

Mike and I, understanding where Jeff's suggestion was headed, hoped for my father's approval as we voiced our excitement.

"I was saving them for the Fourth of July," Jeff added. "Why don't we use them now to blow the nest?"

Dad, trying to look like an adult and act like a parent, said, "Go get them."

I jumped up, shouted incoherently, and slapped Mike's hand. Dad smiled as he continued to empty out the remaining containers on the beach ball-sized beehive. He was looking forward to Jeff's pre-Fourth of July fireworks show just as much as we were.

With an adult's blessing, Jeff heedlessly sprinted across the street and toward his garage for the M-80.

"If you guys knew there was a bees' nest, why were you playing in front of the bush? Do you think that was smart?" Dad asked, as we waited for Jeff to return.

"We didn't know," I lied.

Jeff stumbled back to the group, clearly out of breath, holding an M-80 and a lighter high above his head. "Let's blow this pop stand," he chanted.

Mike and I inched closer to the bush for a better view. Dad took the firecracker and the lighter from Jeff and knelt down beside the bush.

"Here we go," Dad said.

Dad lit the M-80, threw it into the bush, and backed away to stand in line with us. We waited in silence for the explosion. It was so quiet; we could hear the M-80's wick burning. The bees, or hornets, whatever they were, were in for a surprise.

Just then, a tremendous ear-popping explosion shook the earth's foundation as a billow of black smoke spewed out of the bush, engulfing the bees' nest, the bush, the mailbox, and most importantly, the wiffle ball. A mushroom cloud developed overhead as bright red flames danced wildly at the epicenter of the explosion. The flames reached heights that shocked even the most complacent neighbors.

Dad didn't know what to do. He joined me, along with Mike and Jeff, as we stared wide-eyed and openmouthed at the growing fireball in sheer amazement and admiration.

A crowd of neighbors scurried from all directions and gathered in the center of the cul-de-sac to watch the blaze. The neighbors were describing the deafening detonation that shook their respective houses to one another; however, nobody was taking any action to put the fire out. The flames mesmerized the growing congregation. The entire cul-de-sac was almost filled to capacity with astounded onlookers.

"The hose!" Dad yelled to those hypnotized by the fire.

The command was fruitless because, at that moment, two fire trucks sped up the block to put the blast out.

I looked at Jeff and smiled as the firefighters soaked the troublesome area with pounds of pressurized water. The entire incident commenced because a bee stung Jeff. I found that mildly amusing, enough so to warrant a smile and half a chuckle. A valuable lesson had been learned by all. Illegal explosives and six cans of flammable bug spray are not a good combination, but surely entertaining.

As the assembly filed out of the cul-de-sac, respects were paid to what was left of the bush and the mailbox, which wasn't much, considering that the firefighters battled the fire's fierce flames for over ten minutes before extinguishing it.

The mailbox was melted away. The bush was burned to a crisp. Its roots were all that was left of the once prosperous, ball-hogging bush. However, our bee problem was solved … forever.

Dad always said that he hoped a few bees were left alive. "The ones that escaped can warn others that we don't fool around in this neighborhood," he told us.

The mailbox was eventually replaced, and the bush had incredibly survived and flourished, flaunting its fantastic yellow flowers, daring bees to return. I never recognized how beautiful a bush it was until after it had been through hell. Its true colors had been revealed through adversity.

Dad and I were the last to leave the scene. As we walked together in silence past the burning bush and into our garage, we noticed that Rob was sitting in the back of our parked car with his hands over his ears.

"The thunderstorm is over," Dad said to my brother. "You can come out now."

♦   ♦   ♦

Dad was wrong. The bees had returned. The space around my head was teeming with them, but I wasn't afraid. Somehow, I knew they weren't going to sting me. I robotically knelt down, stuck my hand into the bush, felt around, and pulled out a perfectly scuffed wiffle ball.

"I found it!" I exclaimed. It only took until a day after my passing.

I took the ball, ran into the center of the cul-de-sac, and faced the open mailbox as a pitcher stares down a clean-up batter with the game on the line. As I practiced my pitching motion, I imagined I was on the mound at a sold out Yankee stadium in the bottom of the ninth inning of game seven of the World Series.

It must be an unusual sight to see a grown man standing alone in the middle of the street rehearsing his pitching delivery to the mailbox. However, at that moment, I didn't feel like an adult. I was still a kid, and I wouldn't be so sure that if any of my neighbors were watching me through their windows, they too wouldn't see me as a child.

When Jeff and I were children, we would compete to see who could throw a wiffle ball into the small 3x5 opening in the mailbox. The first one to succeed would win a free lunch in town. It was a near impossible feat.

We tried every day for an entire summer, but we never had a chance to hear the plastic ball rattle around the metallic interior of the letterbox. We equated this to scoring a hole in one in golf.

It wasn't meant to be.

After thirty years, I wanted another chance at that free lunch. I looked around for a witness, but unfortunately, I was all alone in the middle of the street.

I still had an urge to give the near impossible toss one last try even if I had no one to share the experience with.

"Here goes nothing," I said to myself.

I set at the belt, wound up, and fired an overhand curve ball directly into the center of the mailbox, for the first time ... ever.

The ball curved straight into the center of the opening without the help from any ricocheting bounces off the sides of the mailbox, like a rimless swish shot in basketball. I couldn't believe it. I did it. Even though nobody was there to vouch for my accomplishment, it was still a sweet moment. It was worth all of the practice throws and uneventful competitions against Jeff for the one time to actually see the wiffle ball fly into the mailbox and stay there. It was truly an exhilarating feeling, and I sensed that it could have only happened at that moment, and not a second before ... or after. I was quickly learning that that was how things worked where I was, on the other side.

"Lunchtime!" my mother shouted from the house. I swirled around to catch up to my spinning head. *Could it be ...*

"Mom?" I said dubiously.

I was instinctively drawn to her. I passed the mailbox and floated across the front lawn as I listened to Mom sing my favorite lunch song.

> *Peanut, peanut butter, and jelly,*
> *Peanut, peanut butter, and jelly,*
> *First you take the peanuts and you spread it,*
> *You spread it, you spread it, spread it, spread it ...*

I was being enticed away from my mission by my mother's music, same as how Odysseus was tempted off-course by the sweet luring songs of the sirens in the sea, and I didn't care. I didn't want to travel into the unknown anymore. I wanted to stay where I felt most comfortable. Even if it was just an illusion taking me deeper into the abyss or the devil in drag taking me further away from my brother, I wanted to let my memories win me over and take me to my rightful resting place. I wanted to be home.

To hell with my brother, I concluded. *Let him find his way back by himself.*

> *Who wants to have some Cheerios?*
> *Cheerios, Cheerios,*
> *Who wants to have some Cheerios?*
> *Earl-y in the morning?*

I kicked my shoes off and sprinted across my childhood's front lawn, passing the Sycamore's two-person tree house along the way. It had been a long time since the bare bottoms of my feet kissed the earth's grassy surface. Running barefoot was something that I did often as a child, but it was an activity that I never could get away with as an adult. I loved it when blades of grass tickled the bottoms of my feet, and when the thin coating of dirt between my toes dried up and crusted into a hard shell along the surface of my skin. However, they were both feelings that I had no other choice but to grow out of and substitute with more mature, adult-like sensations such as responsibility, cleanliness, and rationality. I went from getting my feet dirty by becoming one with my natural environment, to getting my hands dirty by pushing papers in a cold drafty office seventy-two floors up from any rich fertile soil. Moreover, as the years slowly drifted by along the predictable banks of a chartered river, no matter how grounded I would become, there would always be the rubber soles of my shoes to put some distance between myself and the very essence of my being. Never would the bottoms of my feet be branded again with the washable tattoo of life.

I was growing up. I was wearing shoes all of the time. I was dying.

But, at that moment, I wasn't grown up anymore. I also wasn't wearing any shoes. I was already dead. I was three steps away from my mom. She stopped singing and gave me a dirty look as she sat on the front porch.

I stopped short.

What did I do now?

"Did you tell Robby it was lunch time?" Mom asked.

My mouth fell open. *Did she say Rob?* Hopeful thoughts sprung into my head like a dehydrated frog leaping into pond.

Maybe he was here all the time and I wasn't looking hard enough?

"Where is he?" I asked.

"Over there," she said, pointing straight ahead toward the cul-de-sac.

"Really?" I stuttered. I shot Mom a confused glance before apprehensively turning around to face the cul-de-sac.

I almost collapsed. I clutched onto the porch to break my fall.

"It can't be," I whispered fearfully.

Right in the middle of the street, near my imaginary pitching mound, sat my grandmother's shed; its front door was flapping in the still air.

As I stood in-between my late mother, who was sitting on the very deck where I shared my first kiss with Kim Kapler from down the block, and the dreaded shed, which housed some of my most painful memories, I knew it was now time to make my decision between my heaven and my hell.

"Don't just stand there," Mom voiced. "Get Robby so we can all have lunch together. I etched a secret message into the peanut butter for you guys, but you can't read them until you get Rob."

I thought she didn't want me to go near the shed?

When we were at my grandmother's house, Mom was just as much of a staunch antagonist against my decision to rescue my brother as the rest of the family was.

What made Mom change her mind?

I was stuck between two opposing poles of a magnet, one ensuring me the security of the known and the other taunting me with the ambiguity of the unknown. My midnight hour was fast approaching, but nevertheless, my mind was made up long before the attraction and distraction between good and evil would confront me.

I was to bring my brother home. I sat on the ground and tied my shoes with a double knot. My confidence was relentless. I turned to my mother, and I knew by the expression on her face that I wasn't going to be alone on this journey.

I left my mother and approached the shed. Even though it was not raining on the steps of my childhood house, I noticed a torrential rainfall pounding the shed, and only the shed, not unlike my last road trip with Rob, leaving a swollen puddle in front of the shed door.

I reluctantly remembered how my grandparents' backyard always had poor drainage, and whenever it rained, the water would collect to form a moat of bacteria in front of the shed door. To the unprepared warrior, it might have seemed an almost impossible obstacle to pass. Even though no one would take such a risk in order to reach the contents of the shed, be it a couple of boxes of Christmas lights, some old-fashioned outdoor toys, and rusted implements of landscaping, I had been trained for this leap my whole life.

There was something that I needed from that shed, which was much more meaningful than the usual box of broken Christmas lights. I backed up three steps.

Everything is done for a reason.

Now I know why Uncle Ricky made me practice jumping, I concluded. *I had been in training my whole life.*

With my knees bent, my eyes fixed, and my soul determined, I rocked.

One ... two ...

"Watch out for the bees," I heard a child's voice scream out.

I knew exactly who it was.

"Mike!" I exclaimed. "What are you doing here?"

Mike and Jeff rode their bikes up to the top of the cul-de-sac. Even though it was great to see my best friends again, I was shocked. *Were they really here or was this just another imaginative obstacle keeping me from my task?*

There was no way I could possibly see them unless they were dead or were fabricated by my imagination to help allay my nerves as I approached my final destination. But, then again, even if they weren't dead in a physical sense, they were, for all intents and purposes, dead to me in a spiritual sense since we had disconnected our line of communication twenty years ago.

That's what time does. It's a subtle relentless push away from the comfortable and toward the unknown. And we're all contagious to its never-ending ticks, marching us into forced adaptation.

Mike, Jeff, and I were inseparable between the ages of six and sixteen. Even though it helped that our houses were only fifty feet apart from each other, we innately enjoyed one another's company. In the summer, when we weren't wreaking havoc together in school, we played out in the street from the sun stained dawn to the darkness of night, only to break for lunch and dinner. Games like box ball, football, basketball, cricket, and especially wiffle ball, were our favorite afternoon activities. We also filmed movies together with my dad's camcorder, and even frequented the golf course so I could flex my muscles in my dominant sport.

Everything was perfect and none of us wanted anything to change, but we couldn't run around the cul-de-sac invincible, innocent, and worry-free forever, as the hands of time ran around in an endless loop.

Time had different plans for us in the future.

Unlike my friends, it was slightly harder for me to understand the nature of time, and I clung onto artifacts from the past to try to counteract the inevitable changes that I would eventually be forced to make thanks to the insistently continuous compulsory march, but it was a losing battle.

When it was time for college, Jeff and Mike both voluntarily left the unforgettable games of ghost in the graveyard, the annual marathon charade contests against opposing blocks, and the daily neighborhood bike rides along the Hudson to live on campus at their respective universities and welcome a new era into their responsive lives. I, on the other hand, stayed at home and commuted to school, hoping to preserve the past and ease into the untested future. I felt more comfortable slowly peeling away at the stubborn Band-aid masking my vulnerability. Jeff and Mike preferred to yank theirs off with one clean swipe.

It wasn't as if we never saw one another again. We were still best friends, even though we weren't around each other every day anymore. I made sure it was just like old times whenever they returned home for holidays and summer vacation.

All things considered, time had affected the bond between us only slightly. Nevertheless, like a rolling stone, time builds on its own momentum and exponentially gets stronger as it collects everything in its all-encompassing path.

After college, Jeff and Mike both got full-time jobs and moved off the block. I fought the urge for change and lived with my parents for a few more years while still striving to stay one step ahead of time.

No matter how fast I ran, I couldn't outrun the clock.

Now, as if we were young again, Mike and Jeff were offering me a chance to go back home or home as they imagined me imagining it.

We were once best friends. Inseparable. We were now distant strangers. The mailbox game, ghost in the graveyard, and the burning bush were things of the past. But, there was no more time. The rolling stone was covered with moss and had skidded to an abrupt stop.

When there is no more time to battle, you can once again live invincible, innocent, and worry-free. In heaven, you are once again a child.

"Don't worry," Jeff sneered. "There's no dogs where you are going. We know how you're allergic to them." They both laughed as they stopped their bikes right in front of my laces. Neither of them gave as much as an awkward glance at the mysterious shed before us. It was as if its presence in the middle of the street was simply just another unsuspecting patron of the block.

"I have to go right now," I said. "I have to go get my brother." I pointed to the shed. "He's in there."

Jeff and Mike followed my finger's direction and turned to the shed.

"How did that happen?" Mike asked.

"You're not really thinking about going in there, are you?" Jeff inquired.

"He's my brother," I replied, rather annoyed. "Isn't the answer to your question a no-brainer?" I wasn't about to let them steer me off-course. They saw the shed all along. Heaven's final defense mechanism now disguised itself as my best friends, and was doing everything that it could to prevent me from escaping the pure side, even going so far as to initially discredit the existence of its antithesis.

"Nobody comes back," Jeff said in my father's voice.

"Remember, Jason. Years ago, we dared him to go in there for ten minutes … and he still hasn't come out."

"Easy does it," I heard Uncle Ricky coach. "Bend your knees and push off."

I conceptualized my grandmother's bush sitting in front of the shed instead of the pool of water to help me with my jump. Confidence suddenly rushed through me as I substituted the unknown for the familiar. All of a sudden, the jump didn't appear as taxing.

As I soared over the bush, or pond, whatever it really was, heaven's two border control officers, at one time my best friends, watched in stunned silence, defenseless to my escape. There was no doubt in my mind that I was going to make it across, and all that I could think about as I prepared to stick my landing was how I went through painstaking efforts during my life to preclude myself from being lured into the very gates of hell that I was struggling to enter at that seminal moment.

All the praying. All the giving. All the worshipping. Was it all in vain? I asked myself. *Maybe this is my destiny.* But predetermination was never my dig. I always believed that we controlled our own fate. If I didn't, then the decision to save my brother from preordained doom to reverse his own fate would be completely futile and irreparable. *I want to believe that I have complete autonomy over my future or else my journey into the shed has nothing to do with my choices,* I feared.

I stuck the landing on the wooden walkway directly in front of the open shed door. Without a stamped passport, visa, or bell, book, or candle, I carried my brother's Power Ranger's book bag full of monster meat into my grandmother's shed, which sat in the middle of my childhood cul-de-sac, as my dead friends beckoned me not to enter.

Maybe I should have listened.

6

MR. HENDERSON

"Robby!" my grandmother yelled from her front yard. "Mr. Henderson's here."

I sat across from Rob in my grandmother's kitchen as we finished the last of my 'lucky' thirteen-year-old chocolate birthday cake in silence.

I curiously and suspiciously studied his ghost-white stoic complexion wondering when he was going to acknowledge my birthday.

What's with him today?

Rob had been acting strange all day ever since Mom and Dad dropped us off at Grandma's house for an impromptu sleepover weekend. He kept mostly to himself, and was shivering on the car ride down, even though it was one of the muggiest, most sultry days of the year.

I thought he was just trying to ruin my first teenage birthday and I resented him for his bizarre attention-grabbing behavior.

Some brother, I mused.

"Robert!" Grandma yelled into the house, this time with more potency and conviction. "He's waiting for you to come out."

Something was definitely bothering my brother. He began blinking iteratively as he slowly picked at his half-eaten slice of cake. The mouse crumb portions that rode the tottering forklift to his usually amenable palate had a hard time making their way down his digestive roller coaster. He winced with every bite as if he were eating something painfully sour.

The three pieces I had eaten, however, tasted quite pleasant, and I couldn't understand why he was attacking his plate so apprehensively.

Just then, the dizzy modicums of bedraggled chocolate and flour saliva reversed their paths down the inside of the small intestine, compelling Rob to spit up my birthday cake, along with his own bile, and the remaining un-evacuated eggs he had for breakfast, right into his plate and all over his shirt.

"Are you okay?" I asked uneasily.

The front screen door snapped inward, slowly hissed its way back home, and clapped against the wooden doorway a few times before settling to rest. I always associated the sounds of the screen door closing after being disturbed by a trespasser with the ambiance of summer, which put me at ease and made me feel very comfortable. Rob, on the other hand, must not have felt the same way.

The door's final exhale made Rob shudder.

Or was it the intruder that gave him all of this anxiety?

Judging by the *bassy* timbre of the intruder's methodical footsteps, I deducted that they weren't being made by my grandmother.

"I want to go home!" Rob cried.

Mr. Henderson brought the deep pounding footsteps into the kitchen and smiled amicably as he chewed on a two-week old wad of tobacco. The colorful tattoos cloaking his muscular arms, along with his well-proportioned giant stature, would make any pre-teen child nervous. But underneath his imposing shell was the nicest and friendliest person in the world.

Even though he appeared a little rough around the edges, discounting his smooth bald head, my grandmother had no complaints having him as a next-door neighbor because he never bothered anybody for anything during the twenty-five years he made across the street his home, and he was always exceptionally pleasant around her grandchildren.

Mr. Henderson lived by himself, rarely leaving the confines of his home. However, he had a particularly close relationship with my brother, which was why I couldn't understand the reason for Rob's unusual reaction to his sudden presence that day.

Every time we would visit Grandma, Mr. Henderson and my brother would escape to the shed for hours and work on building a model B-52 Bomber airplane. It was the same plane that Mr. Henderson served on as a bombardier during The Vietnam War. Mr. Henderson's plane had been shot down over Hanoi during the famous Rolling Thunder campaign, and was taken captive and tortured as a prisoner of war for six years.

Mr. Henderson managed to escape, but his captivity made him bitter, and he never stopped blaming America for his ordeal.

Grandma believed that he was constructing the model to face his demons and accept his past.

"Sometimes it takes a lot of scratching and scraping to dig to the bare core of one's true emotions," Grandma explained. "And most of the time, what you'll find below the superficial surface is the source to all of your misplaced sentiments ... yourself."

Whenever Mr. Henderson came over for dinner, he would tell us jaw dropping war stories, and rant about the destructive nature of the government.

"Big brother lied to me," he would scream across the table, pounding his fists down until the utensils jumped with fear. "Never trust big brother," he would continue. "He'll forget about you when you need him the most."

Grandma would always roll her eyes and try to kindly change the topic of conversation to something much less interesting. Rob, on the other hand, would look at me and sigh. I hoped my sibling understood that Mr. Henderson wasn't being literal when he said not to trust big brother.

It was always a very humorous dinner scene whenever he was around. However, being a passive supporting actor to Mr. Henderson could also get very exhausting and overwhelming; especially by the time he was rejuvenated with his first cup of coffee. Dessert time was also show-and-tell time, Grandma's favorite time of the night. Mr. Henderson would astound Grandma by presenting her with the previous night's additions to the model B-52 while Rob would sit in silence picking at his cupcake.

"Last night, Rob helped lay the wing dowels on the wing saddle," Mr. Henderson would say, as he presented the incomplete model to my grandmother.

Grandma would always be so genuinely impressed with the progress.

"You built this, Robby?" Grandma would ask proudly. "You're doing such a good job. I can't wait to see what it looks like tomorrow."

"When we're done," Mr. Henderson would remind my grandmother while smiling at my brother, who continued to sit detached, "Rob wants to give it to you as a gift for letting him stay up so late to work on it."

"I'm honored," Grandma would exclaim, as she kissed Rob's forehead, leaving a faint rim of lipstick below his hairline. "I'm so proud of you."

I sorely desired a compliment like that from Grandma. Rob didn't know how lucky he was. Instead, he just sat there as though he were half-asleep.

Rob was never too tired to join Mr. Henderson in the shed though no matter how late show-and-tell time ran. Sometimes Rob would not return from the shed until late at night when everyone, including myself, was asleep.

I was more jealous of their relationship than curious. I would have loved an invitation to the shed, but I was too proud to ask for one. Besides, Rob would beg me not to go with them.

"Don't follow us," he often told me.

I thought he was simply being an asshole for selfishly hogging the limelight, but I would always respect his uncultivated pleas because they sounded eerily genuine and forewarning.

"Hi, boys," Mr. Henderson said, as he walked up to and stood over Rob who nervously wiped the vomit away from his mouth and cowered in the guest's shadow. "Ready to go, Rob? We've got the left wing to paint today."

Mr. Henderson sounded impatient, but still appeared both upbeat and excited, which ironically complemented Rob's awkward cake-upchucking behavior quite well.

"Rob's not feeling too well," I told Mr. Henderson. "I'll help you paint the wing today. It's my birthday you know." I felt like this was my chance finally to get in on the top-secret construction project in the shed.

Mr. Henderson smiled and placed his hand onto Rob's shoulder as he stared directly into the sick nine-year-old's sullen eyes, their faces two nose-lengths apart from one another.

"Don't be ridiculous," Mr. Henderson replied, squeezing my brother's shoulder tightly. "Robby looks fine."

Mr. Henderson released Rob's shoulder from the trained war veteran's grip, covered his hand over Rob's furrowed forehead, and smirked.

The examined shivered fearfully.

"No fever either," the examiner concluded. "Now, how can you have the chills without having a fever?"

He was belittling the already derogated boy.

"I can do it," I promised. "I love airplanes. I was on an airplane when we went to Disney World last summer for vacation."

"No!" Rob screamed. "I'll go," he succumbed, declining my invitation.

I was furious. I couldn't understand why I wasn't allowed to fill in for my brother when he wasn't feeling well.

Both Rob and Mr. Henderson didn't want me with them in the shed, and I suspected they both had different reasons for my nonattendance.

"See," Mr. Henderson said through his smile. "Robby's a trooper. We don't need your help."

My grandmother's hermit neighbor playfully rubbed Rob's hair before standing back up to once again ruffle the sleeping front screen door.

"Let's go," he motioned for my sick, terrified brother.

"I'll be right back," Rob murmured unwillingly. "I need to get something first."

Rob walked passed me in the kitchen, dragging his feet along the way. As our paths crossed, he turned to me and whispered wearily, "Happy Birthday," as if his gift to me that year was the charitable deed of declining my bid to the shed.

He wiped his eyes, turned his back on me, and trudged up the steps.

He has some nerve, I thought. *He had all day to wish me a Happy Birthday. Why did he wait until now? He's rubbing it in that I'm not invited.*

I didn't even want to go with them anymore. My birthday was ruined. Mr. Henderson hardly acknowledged my presence, and my only brother refused to wish me a heartfelt birthday greeting without teasing me for not being welcomed into the shed. All I wanted to do was go to sleep so my day in the sun could end more quickly.

Lucky thirteen wasn't so lucky after all.

Looking back, I should have recognized the warning signs, but I was a poor judge of character as a nubile thirteen-year-old, and I was even less skilled at interpreting people's behavioral patterns. My brother's silent treatment during the car ride down to Grandma's, his plate of half-eaten, half-digested cake, his lurid complexion in the face of Mr. Henderson, his trembling vocal texture, and his blatant disregard of my birthday were all apparent clues to his true intentions for keeping me away from the shed. I egoistically misconstrued my brother's evidence to land a premature conviction for my dreadful birthday.

I was once again only thinking of myself.

It wasn't until Rob returned from upstairs with the show stopping evidence to convince me to reopen the case and reinterpret my brother's odd behavior.

He came bouncing down the steps wearing his Power Ranger book bag. "I'm ready," he told Mr. Henderson with his head lowered shamefully.

Something's wrong, I inferred. *Why else would he need his lucky knapsack?*

"It's about time," Mr. Henderson replied.

The extravagantly comfortable neighbor placed his arm around Rob, and the two of them left me to celebrate my birthday alone. I tried to ask Rob non-verbally about his reasons for bringing his book bag before he exited the kitchen, but my attempts to capture his attention were ineffective.

I concluded that Rob was no longer to blame for my less than perfect birthday. For some reason, Rob thought that he may have needed the magic possessed in his book bag for the night with Mr. Henderson in the shed, and if that was the case, then he had a lot more uncomfortable things on his mind than to remember to wish me a Happy Birthday. I forgave him for his seeming insolence.

Instead of investigating, I respected my brother's request to keep me away from the shed, and I washed up for an early sleep.

"It's probably nothing serious," I told myself. "What's the worst that can happen? Mr. Henderson's there to chaperone."

◆   ◆   ◆

Eleven thirty P.M. My plan to end my birthday early was foiled by insomnia. I was forced to experience every waking second of day one of year thirteen. I reposed impatiently in my grandmother's guest bedroom—which used to be my dad's room growing up—for my brother to return from the shed. I had so many questions to ask him and I didn't think that I could hold out until morning.

The bedside alarm clock noted another passing minute. Eleven thirty-one P.M. Rob and Mr. Henderson had been in the shed for over five hours. I could have painted both wings of a real 747 jet in that stretch and still had time to wash most of the windows.

The bedroom door creaked open. It was so dark I might as well have had my eyes closed, but with my other senses compensating for the blinding blackness of night, I was easily able to discern that the invisible figure tiptoeing his way across the room and over to the pullout bed was Rob.

Past his bedtime, I thought, as the clock struck 11:32 P.M.

I was annoyed that he could get away with his late nights without punishment.

I was jealous that I wasn't a VIP to his club.

I was about to begin my barrage of questions, but before I could gather my thoughts, I was interrupted by the sounds of my brother sobbing.

As he attempted to silence his recalcitrant sniffles, I wondered what could have happened in that shed.

What should I do? Should I console him?

His cries were becoming more painful to listen to, but instead of taking action, I continued to make believe that I was asleep. Rob's increasingly loud sobs scared all of my sheep away for counting. Sleep was no longer a viable escape from my brother's weeps. Whatever happened in the past five hours, Rob had been reduced to a quivering baby. As I fought tears of my own, I was determined to find out the truth behind my brother's late night extravaganzas.

I was determined to follow them into the shed.

◆   ◆   ◆

There are some memories that are better off forgotten … some experiences that are not worth revisiting. But, as I bravely stood inside my grandmother's shed for the first time since my fatal car crash, I knew that I had once again followed my brother into an experience that would have fried the circuits of the most powerful computer.

I had walked back into the nightmarish memory of that stormy night when I gathered the courage to follow Rob and Mr. Henderson into the shed. My own built-in computer had opted to delete this corrupt file from the hard-drive before it caused a system failure. Somehow, the file was recovered in death, and its continuous playback was causing my featureless monitor to freeze in fear.

I scanned my surroundings and became alarmingly uncomfortable. A dusty tool bench collected spider webs near the back wall of the shed. An incomplete set of golf clubs rested underneath the table along with a spinning bike wheel and a semi-built model airplane. The sight of the fallen plane made me quiver.

All of the obscure footprints in sand that I laid out over the beaches of time, which were gracefully washed away by the moon's dance with the earth's tides, were now magically reappearing to guide me.

I hid behind a rotted unhinged wooden door by the far corner of the shed and waited for my brother and Mr. Henderson to enter … just as my thirteen-year-old counterpart did over thirty years ago.

I hoped that this rescue mission would be far less traumatizing than the last.

Just then, a giant woodchuck scurried out from underneath the tool bench, knocking into the bike wheel as it frantically made its way out of the front door. The oversized rodent caused me to jump back in fear, surprising me like an unexpected cheaply placed shrewd sound in a poorly made horror movie.

During the summer of my fifteenth birthday, that very same woodchuck lived out of my grandmother's shed, and every morning would venture over to the house and gnaw at the wooden garage door like a devil's apostle stealthily escaping the depths of hell to destroy the sanctuary of my home. The demonic woodchuck almost made it all the way through the wood to sacrilegiously enter our house, but Uncle Michael protected the sanctity of the home by throwing down a bag of blessed mothballs near the gnashed-up garage door to expel the disguised devil.

Where are Rob and Mr. Henderson?

My question was immediately answered, as I heard a pair of footsteps making their way to the shed. I pulled a kitchen knife out of my pocket and waited quietly behind the inactive door in the darkened corner for their presence, this time around, knowing exactly what to expect.

◆   ◆   ◆

"Did you finish building the airplane last night?" I curiously asked Rob, as I scratched the cue ball into the side pocket.

I was trying to circumspectly investigate my brother's continuously tumultuous demeanor without scaring him more than he already appeared to be.

Rob chalked the tip of his pool stick and elevated himself onto a small stepping stool so he could better reach the table's felt surface. As he lined up his shot, his hands began to shake, causing the stick to wobble.

He was obviously affected by my question. "We have more to do tonight," Rob revealed, as he muffed his shot.

I circled the pool table and tapped the four ball into a corner pocket, eyeing Rob carefully the entire time. As the cue ball drew back to perfectly set up my next shot, my mind was unfortunately drawing a blank with my follow-up question.

My plan was to run the table with my well thought out interrogation, but I forgot my line of questioning, and I was forced to play the rest of the guessing game conservatively. I couldn't look ahead to the magic eight ball just yet for all of the answers. The field was still open, and I needed Rob's help clearing some of the obstacles standing in the way of the final solution before I could deposit the eight ball's prognostications in my side pocket and use it to help my brother's woes.

"Can you call Mom and Dad and ask them to pick us up today instead of tomorrow?" Rob asked tearfully.

I banked the fifteen ball into the far left corner pocket. Another sound shot, but my thoughts were overly consumed with a different game, separate from the ball breaking table sport in front of us.

He was racking my brain with his downtrodden anemic appearance.

He wanted Mom and Dad to leave their weekend vacation a day early to take us home. *Something must be really serious,* I finally understood.

"I'll call them," I lied. There was no way that they were going to leave the Hamptons a day early. I needed to come up with another plan, and fast, to help my brother, a plan without involving our easily worked-up and overly dramatic parents. I had to take matters into my own hands.

I inadvertently shot out of order and scratched the eight ball. I lost the game to Rob, and he didn't even make a single shot. I never liked that rule. You could do most of the work, make one little mistake, and still come out on the short end of the stick, but those were the rules, and that was life.

"Come on," I urged Rob on. "Let's go wash up for dinner."

◆   ◆   ◆

"Robby!" Grandma panicked, as she scampered apprehensively from the dining room to the kitchen and back again. "Where are you?" she hyperventilated.

Mr. Henderson calmly paced by her side.

"Mr. Henderson's here!" Grandma continued.

I backed into the corner of the kitchen and watched Grandma's frenzied search for Rob with astute anguish. I wanted to clue her in on his whereabouts, but any disclosure would have ruined my fail-safe plan.

"Have you seen your brother?" she asked me.

"I'll check upstairs," Mr. Henderson interjected. He methodically climbed the steps with suspicious composure.

I had to act fast before Mr. Henderson found my brother's hiding place.

As Grandma inspected ill-conceived areas of the extension for a human being, such as under the sofa cushions and inside the fireplace, I quietly opened up the kitchen drawer behind

me and pulled out a steak knife. I examined the utensil carefully as I closed the drawer by leaning my back against it.

"I'll check for him outside," I yelled up to Grandma.

I placed the knife in my jeans pocket as if it were the cast-
about eight ball's magic answer to all of Rob's problems, and I
walked toward the front door with a definite purpose.

I heard Mr. Henderson's footsteps add superfluous strain to
the creaky wooden floor right above my head, and I knew that
with every step, he was closer to finding my brother's temporary hiding spot.

I'm running out of time, I feared.

As the screen door grumbled over its latest disturbance, I
decided to sprint across the lawn, through a light rainfall, and
into the shed, uninvited.

From behind my grandmother's old bathroom door, I
waited for Rob and Mr. Henderson to enter, all the while
clutching the handle of the knife in my pocket, hoping that it
carried the answers … hoping that I wouldn't have to use it
for its natural purpose.

If the pocket-sized prognosticator were really a magic eight
ball, it would have inauspiciously warned, "Outlook not so
good." Though I would have shook some sense into the
rotund fortuneteller and hoped for a better prognosis.

Instead, I waited.

And waited.

Thunder chimed overhead. *We're in for a wet one,* I forecasted.

There was that predictably bad horror movie again. Timely
thunder and lightning at the climactic plot point. I had to

keep reminding myself that I wasn't in a movie, and that the approaching storm was nothing more than a strange coincidence.

I heard voices.

Even though I feared the worst, I didn't know what to expect from my late night snooping. For all I knew, mending a miniature fuselage over Mr. Henderson's melodramatic war stories would be the only thing I would witness.

I felt like I was playing ghost in the graveyard with my friends, battling the urge to break free from restrained hibernation. Even with the slightest movement, I would expose myself to the approaching taggers getting warmer and warmer with every inspection of my isolated hiding area.

Remaining calm was the name of the game.

Being caught in the shed, however, would produce much greater repercussions than being tagged in an innocent game of hide-and-seek. *This is what I've been gearing up for after years of dominating ghost in the graveyard.*

This was no movie. This was no game.

"Don't hide from me ever again," I heard Mr. Henderson reprimand my brother, as they approached the shed's entrance. "Now you don't want your sweet old grandmother getting any crazy ideas, would you?"

"I was looking for my book bag," I faintly heard my brother respond over another, more confident, rumble of thunder.

I wanted to scream out, "Olly olly oxen free," and end the game that I wasn't even asked to play. I wanted to make an all out dash to home base.

The shed door swung open. The light rain appeared steadier and more suicidal than before, but it wasn't the rain that caught my eye. I was drawn to the sight of my potential taggers.

Next to the doorway, Mr. Henderson yanked Rob's reluctant arm, pulling him deeper into the shed. For Rob to prefer to remain outside during a thunderstorm, I couldn't imagine what terror awaited us within.

Stay quiet!

Mr. Henderson shoved Rob into a spider web and onto the soiled floor. The web wasn't strong enough to break Rob's fall. My brother used his Power Ranger knapsack to cushion the landing.

The attacker backed into my hiding place, thankfully blocking my view of the terror in my brother's eyes. Mr. Henderson's posterior was within my grasp. I gripped the steak knife tightly and remained immobile.

Stay quiet!

"Put down your purse," Mr. Henderson ordered. "And let's get started. We're already behind schedule because of you."

"Leave me alone!" Rob cried. "Please, leave me alone."

"Get over here, boy," Mr. Henderson growled.

Mr. Henderson was doing something with his hands in front of his body that was making my brother freeze with fear. I needed a better angle. An aerial perspective would have worked best for this particular scene. My inexperienced eyes would have captured all of the action from a safe unexposed distance without having to worry about becoming an unpaid supporting cast member against my will.

I had the best angle all along, cinematographically speaking. The moneymaking shot. The frame that would define the movie's essence. Emotionally speaking, however, I was in hell. Anybody with his or her lens caps screwed on correctly would have stopped capturing the footage and emptied their mental storage facilities of the dailies before it could be edited into sequence, replayed, and remembered forever as a groundbreaking shot in the lexicon of film.

Mr. Henderson removed his belt from his pants and unzipped his fly. Even though I couldn't see the beltless man's face, I imagined he would be grinning devilishly from horn to horn. Without hesitation, he dropped his pants to his ankles and there it was. A close up of a Vietnam War hero's ass with a tattoo above the cheeks which read, "Kiss my."

I wondered if Rob was recording the other angle.

"Why don't you wax the plane's wing before liftoff," the half-naked man said to my quivering baby brother.

What airplane? I was so confused. *Why are Mr. Henderson's pants off?*

Mr. Henderson slowly approached Rob, his buttocks no longer consuming my tainted eyes. My rods and cones received their first good look at Rob since the surprising pants dropping incident. I hardly recognized him. He appeared defeated, lost, and violated. My brother needed help, and his book bag, which he hugged firmly, was not providing the necessary solace.

I pulled the knife out of my pocket as the disobedient neighbor bent down next to Rob, and with his private parts obscenely publicized, Mr. Henderson began unzipping the defenseless boy's pants without verbal and/or written consent.

Rob was stuck between the thunderstorm outside and the high-pressure system swelling in front of him. The two weather patterns were scheduled for a collision, and if so, Rob would be swept away by the imminent perfect storm.

"Please don't," Rob begged.

It was too late. My brother's pants were off. I gasped for air as I sank deeper into the vast ocean of helplessness. The tawdry bangs of thunder muted my brother's screams from being heard by the outside world. I was Rob's only hope, and my sweaty hand soaking the handle of my stolen knife recognized the duress that was placed on me to be my brother's hero. I continued to remind myself to stay quiet, and I waited for the opportune time to make my uninvited presence known.

Even though I had just entered the wonderful world of teen hood, I was still ignorant to the scene before me. I did understand, however, that as Mr. Henderson backed into my unclad brother, it was not a commonplace occurrence.

He's hurting Rob, I conjectured.

Rob's shrieks momentarily subsided. Instead, he winced in pain as Mr. Henderson crawled on top of him and kissed his neck.

I couldn't believe what I was seeing. The time for me to act had come … and passed. I stood behind the door frozen, just as I had done the Halloween night Mongo bullied Rob for his stash of candy.

Everything appeared to be moving in slow motion, and balefully, all sound, except for my deep breathing, had stifled into ghastly silence. It was extremely strange to see the shed's small window illuminate with flashes of lightning without the distress sounds of thunder preceding them.

Thanks to the unexplained silence, I was finally exposed, but it wasn't how I originally planned to reveal myself. As Mr. Henderson rocked back and forth into Rob, I urinated in my pants. The sound of my leaky discharge running down my leg and forming a small puddle on the wooden floor beneath me luckily turned Mr. Henderson's attention away from Rob and unluckily toward me.

I'm involved now!

"Who's there?" Mr. Henderson barked.

I crept out from behind the door and shuddered. I couldn't tell who was more surprised to see me. The knife poked into my thigh, reminding me that it was still in my pocket. I couldn't even cut my dinner steaks correctly, much less puncture a human being, if a proper method truly existed.

"What are you doing here?" Mr. Henderson continued, as he dismounted my brother and approached me. Rob, crying quietly, pulled his pants back on and curled into a ball, embarrassed. I was powerless to communicate.

My naked aggressor smiled as he neared my location. "Wet yourself?" he asked rhetorically. "You want to play with us too?"

I was now looking to Rob for help.

I sorely desired to hear the thunder rip through the flashing sky again because it would signify some semblance of normality. To hear only the forthcoming devil's wise remarks without the accompanying background cacophony was a nightmare.

However, whatever information I lost through my sense of hearing, I gained through my sense of smell. The shed reeked of mold, urine … and death.

Mr. Henderson's penis pointed at me like a cannon to an unsuspecting marching army into enemy territory.

"Leave me alone," I cried out. I had become Rob. I tried to will my brother into action, but all he did was reach into his book bag and search for any magic left inside. He had become me. I stepped backward, directly into my puddle of urine, and shook my head in disbelief to try warding off evil.

"I told you not to come with us to the shed," Mr. Henderson said. I was now within his range. I was one penis length away from my naked neighbor, cornered with nowhere to escape. "Take your pants off," he ordered.

As the pervert lunged toward me, I observed, in the corner of my eye, Rob lift his Power Ranger book bag, with his hand still inside the bag, and point it at Mr. Henderson. *What is he doing?*

All of a sudden, the loudest, ear-splitting blast of thunder emanated from the book bag, shaking the underpinning of the shed like an earthquake registered high on the Richter scale. It caught all of us off-guard, especially Mr. Henderson who staggered backward momentarily before collapsing clumsily to the floor.

He was completely still.

Rob cried madly as I neared the fallen war veteran. Mr. Henderson's eyes rolled over white, his mouth gaped open, and his penis relaxed. Blood trickled out from underneath him and formed a dark red pool around his lifeless body.

He was dead. And I felt no sorrow.

The book bag, I wondered. *It is magic!*

My faith was renewed. I was born again.

All sounds quickly returned to their rightful locale. Thunder once again boomed from the sky instead of from my brother's knapsack. The only thing disrupting normality now was our grandmother's naked neighbor lying dead on the shed floor.

I wanted to run as far away from the shed as I possibly could, and never return. However, I had to first console my shaking brother.

We held each other and cried for what felt like an eternity. When Rob pulled his hand out of his book bag to give me a hug, he revealed the source to the book bag's thunderous power, which magically struck our attacker down.

Pop-Pop's gun, I gasped.

As Rob wrapped his arms around me, the barrel of the magnum felt cold against my neck, sending shivers down my spine.

He protected me, I concurred. *And I was idle when my defenseless brother needed me the most. Some brother I was.*

Rob and I waited for the storm to pass before leaving the shed … for the last time.

"Let's go home," I said.

The nightmare was over.

That was the last time Rob and I touched each other like that again.

7

MYSTERY DOOR

I found myself standing in a puddle of my own urine, again, nearly thirty years later. With whatever energy and sanity I had left, I turned and ran to the shed door and desperately pulled at the knob to set me free.

I was stuck. The door wouldn't budge.

I had a second chance to save Rob from Mr. Henderson's wrath, but I just stood there and watched … again. We could have both been back at Grandma's for Christmas dinner, but once again, because of me, Rob has been driven deeper into the uncharted depths of hell.

"It was self-defense … self-defense!" I screamed, as I pounded the shed door with my bloody knuckles. I thought that maybe I could convince whomever it was that handed down our ultimate judgment to reverse my brother's verdict.

I leaned my back against the door and slid down to the floor, exhaustion and depression became my companion.

I banged my head against the shed door and cried. "It was self-defense," I whispered. "Self-defense."

That was what I remembered the judge decreeing. The robed man talked of Mr. Henderson's semen being found on my brother, which was enough proof for him that the murder was committed in self-defense.

I didn't understand at such an early age what the judge meant. All this time I had thought that Mr. Henderson was in the Air Force. *He must have been in the Navy,* I assumed from all of the references being made of his semen. *I guess you never really know who your neighbors are.*

Even though Rob was a minor, there was a large public outcry for his conviction, on the grounds of killing a Vietnam War hero. In the months following, Rob rarely left his room, and until the day he died, he was never the same.

Our concern for Rob, although always genuinely present, was never more realized until his first day of ninth grade of world history class.

◆   ◆   ◆

His teacher was Mrs. Pratt, a rotund elf-like elderly woman who wore glasses uncomfortably too far down the bridge of her nose. She thought that history was the most important subject in school, and she expected all her students to feel the same way.

"We study history so we don't make the same mistakes twice," she would lecture, always pointing her glasses at her students to the rhythm of every one of her emphasized spoken syllables for dramatic effect.

"History is nothing more than yesterday's news," a bold classmate would shout out, making Mrs. Pratt's face turn red.

"Who cares about the Navajo Indians or the Louisiana Purchase? I want today's headlines."

A remark like that would force Mrs. Pratt to bring out the gavel. She never used it on any of her students, but the threat that her judge's mallet issued always silenced the uproarious gallery.

The first assignment she handed out to my brother's class was a semester long book report and presentation concerning a specific topic in world history. She assigned a different subject to each student on the first day of class, ranging from the Mayan pyramids in Mexico to the collapse of communism in Russia.

"No trading your topic with your friends," Mrs. Pratt explained. "You must report on the topic you are assigned."

As Mrs. Pratt read off the students' names in alphabetical order, followed by their respective semester long historical thesis, Rob sat at his desk and patiently waited for his name to be called, hoping, like the rest of the students, that his topic was something current and interesting.

"Allison … the Boston Tea Party," Mrs. Pratt read. "Craig … the Emancipation Proclamation. David … John Brown's raid."

The students would sarcastically grunt and groan with every topic the stoic teacher would call out.

"Can I do my report on the marriage of Tom Cruise and Nicole Kidman?" a blonde-haired, bubble-chewing girl asked semi-seriously with her hand raised high. Mrs. Pratt almost fell off her chair. The only pop culture that ever made it into her lesson plan was the debate over the pros and cons of the stylish bright red British military outfits during the Revolutionary War.

"Heather … Gandhi's Salt March," Mrs. Pratt continued without denigrating herself to answering the bubbly blonde's outlandish request.

"Rob …"

My brother perked up, awaiting his assignment with quiet anticipation.

"… Operation Rolling Thunder."

Rob's heart changed its time signature and tempo. The once soulful organ was now beating to a different drum, playing more of the blues.

Rob knew exactly what Operation Rolling Thunder was, and how it impacted world history. The air attack had a direct affect on his life also. How could he forget the countless number of times Mr. Henderson recounted his participation in the largest, most destructive air raid in military history during dinner at Grandma's?

"Those Gooks never saw us coming," Mr. Henderson would chant with his mouth full of mashed potatoes. "We dropped over a million tons of bombs on those bastards. Operation Rolling Thunder," he would chuckle. "We not only brought the thunder, we brought the lightning as well."

My brother had conducted all of the research that he ever wanted to do in a lifetime about the ongoing air raids on North Vietnam, and he squirmed uneasily in his chair with his shaking hand raised, desperate to change his topic.

"What is it, Rob?" Mrs. Pratt asked, annoyed. She didn't know whether to reach for the gavel or her glasses. She went for both.

"Can I have a different topic?" Rob responded over a disgusted sigh.

"What did I say earlier?" the impatient teacher scolded. "Do you think the rules don't apply to you?" Mrs. Pratt shook her head unappreciatively and finished reading off her class roster's assigned report and presentation topics.

"Tim ... the Watergate scandal."

If Rob could not convince his teacher to change his topic, then he would be reminded of his greatest nightmare every day for an entire semester. He had to act fast before his mental levee broke beyond repair.

"Excuse me," Rob audaciously said.

"I've heard just about enough out of you," Mrs. Pratt shot back.

Rob was stunned, and with his request denied, his mental dam caved in. As Mrs. Pratt laid out the ground rules for the project, Rob drifted away from the classroom and back into the shed, his teacher's voice morphing into an indistinct echo.

"I want you to become *intimate* with your topic," Mrs. Pratt preached, using her glasses once again to stress certain words. "Know it from the *inside out*. And if you know anybody who has firsthand experience with your topic," Mrs. Pratt continued, "then you should hold a *private* interview with him. I want you to *become* your topic. *Tackle* it."

Rob was interpreting Mrs. Pratt's words a little differently than how she intended them to be construed, and he flipped out. The waters exploded through the barricade and flooded his brain with temporary insanity.

Rob pushed his chair back, stood up, and flipped his desk over. The desk crashed to the floor, spilling everything that was inside of it. He screamed at the top of his lungs, stupefying and silencing the classroom.

Mrs. Pratt had stripped Rob down to his bare, most vulnerable state, just like Mr. Henderson did to him in the shed a couple of years prior. This time, however, he had a much larger audience. All of the eyes were on Rob, including Mrs. Pratt's bloodshot glare. She squeezed the gavel's handle as thoughts of throwing it across the classroom toward Rob's head streaked across her mind.

Rob fell to his knees and sobbed for all to hear.

"Mrs. Pratt," a female classmate blurted out, breaking up the awkward silence. "I'll switch my topic with Rob if that's okay."

His classmates burst into laughter, further destroying the already broken-down boy. Mrs. Pratt tried to control the class with her gavel, but the court was already out of order. Before Rob could be held in contempt by the judge, he ran out of the room, deeply embarrassed.

That was the only time Rob's emotional juices would boil. He learned to control his demons very well after the classroom incident; however, they continued to heat his feelings to a boiling point every day.

Rob carried Mr. Henderson's weight with him for the rest of his life, and it was amazing that he never erupted since.

I had an understandably tough time recuperating also. I accepted that the only chance I had of surviving the incident's lingering effects was to erase it from my memory. I called it, forced amnesia. *Make as if it never happened.* And that was what I did. Rob and I never discussed that night, and we never entered the shed again. I tried my best to return to my normal daily activities, and luckily, it didn't take very long to condition myself into forgetting it ever happened.

It was like a bad dream that felt frightfully real during sleep, which, upon waking, failed to be deposited into the memory bank, and vanished from conscious thought, as if it never occurred. The dreams you wished you had written down before they escaped you.

The shed nightmare did make my unconscious its home, and would frequently stop by during sleep to remind me that it would never really let me forget about that night, even if it didn't affect or remind me when I awoke.

In death, however, my worst nightmare packed up and moved right into the forefront of my waking thought, and everywhere I looked, I was reminded of Mr. Henderson.

That's how Rob must have felt his entire life.

◆   ◆   ◆

"Self-defense," I muttered, as I closed my eyes in an attempt to escape the shed again … my locked cage of despair. There was no doubt; I was trapped in hell.

I fell asleep, hoping to escape my nightmare.

Time to wake up,
Time to wake up,
Time to wake up in the moooooorning!

I woke up, as I did a million times before, to the tune of my mother's favorite morning song. I didn't know how much time had passed, but if I had to guess, I would have assumed that I was asleep for an extremely short time. Maybe no time at all. In the shed, I sensed a disregard for time. The hands of time had been cuffed and stabilized at my most painstaking moment, and there was no way for me to locate the key to my shackles, or to the solitary cell that I so desperately needed to escape.

Ironically, all I ever wished for was to live a life not dictated by a clock or a calendar. That was why I loved baseball so much. Since baseball is the only sport not measured by time, all you have to do is keep the rally alive, and you will survive indefinitely. No two-minute warnings, buzzer beaters, or timeouts to worry about. There is all the time in the world to remain forever timeless in a baseball game, depending upon how well you utilize your outs.

Maybe Rob had the right idea all along when he sprinted off
the mound with the game on the line.

To be timeless is to be relaxed, confident, and comfortable. In the shed, however, I prayed for each passing second because they provided me with hope. Hope for eventuality. Hope for change. Hope to get out of this hell.

Just then, I heard a door creak open. It couldn't have been the shed door because I was still leaning my back against it.

But that's the only door here, I questioned.

I followed the sounds of the mysterious door, and they took me right to the unhinged bathroom door that I hid behind when I should have been saving my brother. There wasn't supposed to be an opening behind the unattached bathroom door temporarily stored in the convenient vacant corner of the shed, and even if there were, it would have led to the unexplored heavily wooded backyard of my grandmother's house, and not to an open one-way road stretching out into the horizon.

The way I had entered the shed was still locked from the outside. I approached the new opening, my way out, with caution. I stepped out of the shed and studied my new surroundings.

Normally, I would have tested the untapped waters a little bit longer before diving into the pool, but considering the circumstances, I would have rather taken my chances below the surface than to remain in the shed.

Fallen leaves crunched under my feet as I walked through a gentle breeze in the cool early twilight sky underneath a full orange moon. It was fall. I sensed the energy of October in the air. It smelled of playoff baseball, light windbreaker jackets, and Halloween.

"Halloween!" I shouted. "Mongo!"

I had to find my brother. He was in trouble.

Behind a nearby willow tree, dancing softly in the wind, sat my white convertible Cabriolet, daring me to drive.

The last time I drove my car was to my death. I was now going to take it for another spin to get my life back. *How ironic!* Something told me that this trip was going to be a lot more painful than the fatal ride upstate for a weekend of golf in the epilogue of my autobiography.

I approached my car like a mosquito to a glowing outdoor bug zapper.

There wasn't a single dent or scratch on the vehicle. I was relieved to observe no other signs that my car had previously crashed. I gave myself the clearance to step inside my car, finally excited to be a part of a piece of my past that provided me with mostly pleasant memories.

After all, it was the only vehicle I had ever owned. It was probably long overdue for an upgrade, but my 1987 Volkswagen Cabriolet carried too much sentimental value for me to part with it.

If I was willing to let go of the past, then maybe Rob and I would still be alive, I shuddered to think.

I ignorantly entered, thinking that I would be perfectly safe behind the wheel of my deathtrap.

I stared out at the open road before me. "Looks like there's only one way to go," I said, stating the obvious aloud to myself.

I hope Rob is down that road.

There was only one way to find out. Besides, anywhere away from the shed would be traveling in the right direction.

I stepped on the gas and headed into

8

THE FORK IN THE ROAD

the unknown.

It felt like six hours had passed as I drove down the same stretch of road, passing what seemed like the same cornfield for countless miles. There were no other cars on the desolate highway to keep me company, no signposts up ahead giving me hope or fear of what possibly amassed on the horizon. Nothing for me to look at other than the aforementioned stalks of corn reaching for the heavens from the desiccated soil of hell like lost souls yearning to find their way.

Children of the Corn *or* Field of Dreams? I wondered. *What type of movie am I driving into?* I had to remind myself that I wasn't in a movie. My adrenaline was pumping. This was no act.

Besides, if this was a motion picture, then I was stuck in the most boring scene of what was turning out to be a mysterious horror flick with no ending.

A lull in the storm.

Total monotony, and with very little hope for a change of scenery.

"That's hell," I cracked, pushing the Cabriolet to a smooth eighty-five miles per hour. The road was curiously scarred with a legion of deep dark skid marks every quarter mile leading into the thick cornfields on both sides. I concluded that in the past, this road was home to either many accidents or a fleet of cars frantically escaping the open road to nowhere. If the latter were the case, then I didn't blame them.

I tried the radio. Static. *Why would it work now?*

I was all alone with my thoughts, which was not a very healthy situation. I had to shake Mr. Henderson from my conscience if I wanted to survive this road trip. I allowed my mind to take a much-needed detour from my usual thoughts and hoped it would invite me to hitch a ride.

And then it hit me.

I was overwhelmed by sorrow. Not necessarily because I was dead, but more so because I left nobody behind that would have sincerely grieved for my loss. *Would my death have impacted anybody?*

My co-workers would have attended my funeral, but it would have been more of an obligation for them than a voluntary act of respect.

I was never married. I didn't have any children. No immediate family, except for my two cats, which I was sure didn't make the procession.

I suddenly suffered feelings of inadequacy as I continued to drive.

I wasted my life, I realized. *I never had to bother myself with making a will.*

I even lost touch with all of my friends.

I wondered what others might have imagined my legacy to be.

Employee of the year and three-time wiffle ball champion, I lamented. *That's my goddamn legacy. For the history books!*

Rob would have attended the funeral, despite my perpetual failure to come through for him in the clutch over the years. *That's one person.*

My cousins may have attended, but I didn't know how they would have found out about my passing unless my secretary researched for any of my surviving family members and contacted them for me.

Let's say they came, I calculated. *That's four.*

Counting my four cousins, and a few of my closest co-workers, I estimated a nine-person turnout for my funeral. And if I didn't kill my brother, I could have reached double digits. With a turnout like that, I may have been able to fake a legacy.

I never realized how insignificant a life I led until I took to the road in pursuit of my trivial existence somewhere deep within the bowels of hell.

My funeral must have been lame. No tears shed. No memories shared.

Maybe a person's worth isn't measured by how many attend the funeral, but instead, by how many welcome that person into death.

"My divine surprise party was hopping with loved ones," I boasted.

I reluctantly presumed I had nothing to worry about concerning my legacy, even if nobody was there to say goodbye to my vessel. My loved ones accepted the space inside what used to make my vessel shine, where time is meaningless, and the possibilities endless.

I didn't attend my vacant funeral, and I left my everlasting party in heaven early … in what appeared to be now a desperate search for an identity.

A meaning. A validation.

I thought I was searching for Rob?

◆   ◆   ◆

I was reminded of the cross-country road trip that I traversed with my brother after he graduated college. We drove from Arizona State University in Tempe, Arizona to our home in Valley Cottage, New York in just six days, stopping only to eat, shit, and sleep; 3,008 miles in a car with a disquieted graduate trying to figure out the next stage of his life before the upcoming summer vacation.

I, too, had not yet settled into my own life, if there is ever such a thing to do, and I hoped that confining myself inside a car with nowhere to go except to follow the open road would point me in some kind of direction.

Uncle Ricky was annoyed with us for rushing home. "You are not missing anything in Valley Cottage that won't be there when you get back," he vented. "Do not shortchange the trip. Step up to the plate and see the country. People your age are hiking the Himalayas."

I agreed with my uncle. It would have been nice to go city hopping for weeks without any regard for time, but both Rob and I were growing disgruntled with the endless fields of corn passing through our windows, and the lack of variety made us long for our comfortable routine.

Corn wasn't what I was searching for when I signed up for the trip. I had no connection to the irregular yellow vegetable.

We could have ventured off the super highway and explored the back roads for our purpose, but with every click on the odometer pushing us closer and closer home, I knew exactly where I was meant to be.

"If you go looking for your own heart's desire, and you can't find it in your own backyard, then you've never really had it at all," I remembered Glinda, the Witch of the North, explain to Dorothy in the Land of Oz.

My favorite movie.

I could have used a pair of ruby slippers because all that Rob and I talked about was how much we wanted to go home.

◆   ◆   ◆

I called our cross-country trip, "The road trip from hell," because we never found what we were looking for.

Except the nation's tastiest baby back ribs in Denver.

Little did I know, I scoffed, as I blasted the air conditioning at my dour eyes to prevent myself from falling asleep at the wheel during my undeniable trip from hell. I was somewhere between my grandmother's shed and the great unknown.

This trip was far worse than the cross-country blunder. Unlike the 3,008 miles between Tempe and Valley Cottage, I was alone, nobody to share the cornfield landscape with, and my destination was uncertain. I had no idea what awaited me. I didn't have the safety net of home welcoming me at the finish line.

And most frightening of all, I forgot what I was searching for.

I was driving through the world's largest lost and found, but I couldn't remember whose souls needed saving. Rob's or mine? I forgot who was sentenced to hell in death and who was rewarded with eternal sunshine in heaven. I felt like a stalk of corn praying to the sky for an answer.

I finally found my connection to corn.

I wished Rob were sitting beside me so I could ask him.

Even though it was difficult for Rob and me to sustain a 3,000-mile long conversation—sometimes our silence bordering on awkwardness—I could have used an extra body in the car to help me navigate through the cornfields of hell.

I should find Rob, I thought. *I hope this road takes me to him.*

My mind was going around in circles. I somehow convinced myself again that I needed to find my brother and bring him home.

I still understood that Rob was the one who was in trouble. However, I wasn't so sure anymore if I was any better off.

I'll worry about myself later.

I slowly pulled up to an abrupt fork in the road, the first permutation on my excursion since I discovered a freeway jutting out the back of my grandmother's shed. I put the car in park and stepped out to study my surroundings. The road split in two and ran parallel to one another for an unforeseen distance.

"Where did this come from?" I asked myself. I peered down both roads, trying to discern which option afforded me with the greatest chance for survival. Both paths, however, appeared eerily similar.

Trying to analyze my decision would be futile, so I took my chances and randomly selected the road to my left.

A quiet breeze rustled the corn; they shivered fearfully. I listened to their indiscernible cries as the wind swept through. They sounded like thousands of pleading voices. Marred, lost, and unrefined. I tried to separate the utterances so I could better grasp what they were saying, but the corn seemed to make more sense as a collective unit. I covered my ears and started singing in order to filter out the cries.

> *Nobody likes me; everybody hates me,*
> *Think I'll eat some worms,*
> *Ooshy gushy worms, big fat worms,*
> *Worms that walk and talk.*

My song wasn't working and my earmuffs were outrageously ineffective. I was scared. I felt like I was being surrounded. I didn't know what the voices were crying about, but if I had to guess, it sounded like a desperate longing for broken dreams. An appeal for redemption. They were getting more pronounced as I circled about, failing to keep my brain from processing the converging sound waves. I nervously hopped back into the car and turned the key in the ignition.

The car didn't start. I tried again.

And again.

The Cabriolet coughed weakly, like a sick old man on his deathbed trying to bark out his final words of wisdom. Every time I tried to breathe life into its motor with a simple twist of the wrist, I failed.

I was grounded and frustrated.

I exhaled uneasily, exited the car, and made my way over to the hood, the wind thankfully dying down and the voices subsiding. I didn't know anything about cars, and I wouldn't know what I'd be looking at if I were to open up the hood and study what was inside. But I thought I'd give it a try anyway.

I popped open the hood. I was right. I would have never expected in a million years to unveil what was hiding underneath my Cabriolet's hood.

Dozens of rainbow colored balloons escaped from their claustrophobic cell and soared high above the cornfields.

I collapsed on the side of the road, refusing to believe my eyes.

The balloons drifted higher, and for a second time, I wished that I, too, were a lighter than air. I envied their freedom. Until then, however, I remained a cornstalk held back by the roots.

Even with my limited knowledge of basic automotive mechanics, I knew that there shouldn't be anything, such as balloons, stuffed inside an engine compartment.

How did they get in there?

I didn't want my question answered.

I interpreted the hoard of balloons I was unknowingly smuggling as a warning sign. They were my first directional road signs that I came across on my trip. They were telling me to turn back.

They already succeeded at stopping my car. The balloons stared down from their lofty perch watching my every move, daring me to continue, hoping I wouldn't.

I rationalized that if someone or something did not want me to continue, then I must have been on the right road. The road to my left, the side I selected to travel before my car broke down, was undeniably the road that yielded my brother's whereabouts.

It smells my fear.

"I am not afraid," I chanted. "I am not afraid."

It would have to do a lot better than to throw a bunch of balloons in my face to scare me at this juncture in my journey.

I'm not afraid of clowns anymore, I laughed, almost taunting my invisible foe.

For the first time, I was ready for the challenges awaiting me down the left side of the fork in the road. Or was I?

I rummaged through the backseat for my brother's book bag. I was hungry for monster meat. With a belly full of my grandmother's homemade chunks of beef, I would feel invincible, my fear completely vaporized, but the Power Ranger knapsack was nowhere to be found. I frantically checked underneath the seats and inside the trunk.

It was gone. *I must have left it in the shed,* I figured.

Without my meat, I felt completely vulnerable, and I reeked of fear. My confidence was shattered. I once again dreaded the road before me, and I wanted to turn back for my favorite meal.

"Ahhhhhh," I screamed. I was nothing without my monster meat. The sound I produced reached a pitch that popped all the balloons.

"I am not afraid," I said, as I slid the key back into the ignition. "I will not beat me." I willed the car to start, and then turned the key, hoping my mind games would succeed at fooling the beholder of my fears. It worked. I brought the car back to life, resuscitating the dying old man, and transforming him into a feral, roaring lion. The radio also screamed back to life. George Harrison's, *Beware of Darkness,* blasted through the car's sound system.

> *Watch out now,*
> *Take care, beware the thoughts that linger,*
> *Winding up inside your head,*
> *The hopelessness around you.*

I preferred the static.

I shut off the radio and drove down the left side of the fork in the road.

I was glad that the road split in two because it authenticated the chances of there being something ahead, which also meant that I was drawing nearer to my brother, and my only concern now was if I chose the correct path. The adjacent road remained parallel. If I wanted to, I could still cut across and change, but there were significantly more tire marks bleeding off my road and into the cornfields, and I supposed that the road that everyone was trying to abscond in the past was probably the road that led to where my brother was imprisoned.

"Mrs. Pratt was right," I said to myself. "It's important to study history because it could help you with your decisions in the future."

I suddenly noticed the once parallel road turning back toward me. "What's it doing?" I asked myself. Then, without any reason, it merged back into the road I was on, becoming, once again, a single paved passage stretching out endlessly. The mysterious fork had lasted no longer than five miles.

I couldn't understand the purpose to the short-lived divergence, but I finally realized that I was on the right road. The only road. It didn't matter which reality in the fork I took after all.

They are all the same if you don't know where you're going.

I wondered how much longer, and even though the road looked the same, I sensed I was about to encounter something. Was I prepared? And if I was prepared, prepared for what? *You can always be prepared, but you never know what for.*

I spotted a figure standing in the distance.

9

JASON

I slowed down as I approached an old, overweight man waving his arms frantically for my attention. As he made his way to the middle of the road, I stopped. I didn't recognize him behind his long, gray, unkempt beard or his rotten cavity packed rows of teeth, which strangely looked like a row of deformed-shaped decaying tombstones, however, I felt like I was driving up to an old friend.

It looked like he had been through hell.

I opened up the driver's side window and noticed he had been crying.

Dark rings stained the circumference of the man's eyes; they complemented his stained, colorless cheeks and his wet, matted, gray hair quite well. He reminded me of an older, less jolly Santa Claus.

He suddenly hunched over and dry-heaved beside my car door. He did not look too healthy, and with a reluctant, closer scrutiny, my unexpected visitor seemed to be decomposing. His left ear appeared slightly weathered … or half-eaten.

We stared at one another for a few beats before I realized the identity of the spot lit figure. I almost jumped out of my seat. "Jason?" I inquired.

I remembered the dare Jeff and Mike proposed to our childhood friend in death. A dare that I was sure Jason regretted accepting.

Nobody comes back from the shed, I recollected my angels' voices chanting.

"Am I glad to see you," Jason coughed. "You don't know how long I've been walking along this road without seeing anybody. Can I get a ride?"

He looked nothing like how I remembered, even though the last time I saw him was over twenty years ago. Death did not treat him well. He was the first person I came across on the other side who was not transformed to his prime.

He was not only dead; he looked dead. That was what we all were, but he was the only one who embodied the spirit.

Maybe the shed hastens the aging process, I surmised. I was too scared to look at myself through the rearview mirror. I didn't want to reflect a not so flattering image of myself. I wasn't prepared for such a surprise.

"Get in," I told him.

Jason resided on the cul-de-sac adjacent to mine. He used to cut through Jeff and Mike's backyard to get to our block whenever we needed another person to make even sides in any of our games. He was the Florence Court alternate if any of the cul-de-sac natives were unavailable to play.

Jason endured a childhood long rite of passage, which included tricks, being teased, and fights in order to be allowed to come play on our cul-de-sac. Most of the time, I was the leader of the pack and the object of his frustration.

I didn't like the idea of inviting an outsider onto our block. I feared for my own status with my neighbors whenever a foreigner was invited to join in. I hated going on family vacations. I dreaded that in my absence, a replacement would do such a good job covering for me while I was gone that I would become obsolete and voted off the block. Therefore, I naturally regarded Jason as one of my enemies, a mild threat, and I let him know I wouldn't go down without a fight.

It started out as innocent juvenile tormenting, but then, Jeff and Mike were slowly becoming good friends with Jason, and they began inviting him to the block, and my jealously made me take it out on Jason.

◆   ◆   ◆

I sat at the end of my driveway tossing rocks into a nearby sewer waiting for everyone to come outside for wiffle ball on a hot humid summer day. It was the kind of day that the cicada bugs would have loved to have emerged early from their seven-year hibernation to enjoy the weather.

I had recently mourned over the repaving of the cul-de-sac. All of the rollerblade skid marks I had left on the street, including all of the steps I had taken over the years during the countless number of games I played on the block's surface was wiped clean as if my permanent mark had never been made. I was afraid that my past was being suffocated by a newly applied, shinier layer of asphalt. My legacy was gone in an instant, like a rapidly dissipating handprint on glass.

I felt like I had lost a piece of my childhood, and it was exhaustive to think that I would have to start from scratch making my mark, knowing full well that one day all of my hard work would once again be paved over.

Ironically, that's how I felt in death, excavating for the branded layers of my buried past, too weary to stigmatize a newly applied layer, hoping to recapture my skeletons before my legacy was forgotten.

I chucked my last rock into the small opening in the sewer when I heard movement within the dense foliage of my neighbor's backyard. My view was partially blocked by the trees; however, I could tell that it was Jason approaching.

Uninvited.

What is he doing here? I thought.

His arm was outstretched and he was walking awkwardly, as if he was being pulled through the backyard. My curiosity peaked as I heard Jason say, "Good boy."

He brought his dog with him.

Jason knew all about my fear of dogs.

As they neared, I heard the four-legged beast panting excitedly as he most definitely smelled my surging fear.

"How dare he," I scowled.

I collected a handful of rocks and quietly approached the invader. I hid behind my neighbor's bush ready for my sneak attack and waited for his arrival.

"Hey, where are you going, Max?" I heard Jason cry out.

He's loose! I panicked.

I dropped my ammunition and sprinted back to my house, screaming my head off the entire way over. I must have looked like a complete idiot, but I was too scared to be embarrassed. And then I heard laughter. *Something's not right,* I intuited.

I stopped halfway down my driveway and spun around, knowing instantaneously that I had been made a fool. Jason, armed without his K-9 best friend, stood in the middle of the cul-de-sac, balled over in hysterics, pointing at me.

He embarrassed me on my own turf. My face was beat red with anger.

Jeff came out of his house from across the street and smiled at Jason's unusually up-beat persona.

"Hey, Jason!" Jeff said excitedly.

"Come over and pet my dog," Jason yelled through laughter, as he phantom rubbed an imaginary dog. "He's right over here."

Jason pointed to the vacant space beside him. No dog.

Jeff joined Jason in the middle of the street and the two of them used my fear as a vehicle for laughter. *Jeff was in on the prank,* I realized.

They were both rolling on the ground, cackling mightily at my unfortunate expense. I wasn't happy.

I didn't know whether I was angrier at Jason for exploiting my fear, or Jeff for conspiring with an outsider to exploit my fear. Somebody was going to pay, and that somebody was Jason.

Fighting went against my nature. I was the smallest kid in my fifth grade class. Whenever we had to line up in descending height order during morning program, which was the principal's favorite method for coordinating her students into lines, I was always at the very end. Height was always a disadvantage, but I would have never used it as an excuse to back out of a fight. I just never had any ferocity in me. Nothing ever irked me to the point of throwing punches ... until the day Jason used my phobia of dogs, and turned my best friend into an accomplice.

I collected a new handful of rocks, selecting only the ones with the most jagged edges, ran up to Jason, and pelted him in the face with each pointy stone. I hit my target with each throw, the last one penetrating his skin. I made him mad.

Whose side is Jeff going to take now? I wondered.

Jason, who would always be three-quarters up the line from my caboose position during morning program, stood up, wiped the blood streaking down his cheek, and chased after me with a look to kill.

I knocked on the door, hoping for somebody to answer, as Jason marched up the steps, cornering me on the dead-end patio. I knocked on the door so hard that I thought I was going to break through the wood. My dad finally unlocked the door and poked his head out, freezing Jason in his tracks before he was able to reach me.

"What's going on?" Dad asked.

Both Jason and I pleaded our cases to my dad at the same time, as Jeff stayed a good distance away from the scene, cowardly refusing to take any sides. We both rambled indiscernible tones, too fast for my dad to process, let alone understand.

"Slow down," Dad said, growing annoyed, momentarily silencing both of us.

"Go run to your daddy for help," Jason teased.

"Jason made believe he brought his dog to scare me, you know, because he knows I'm afraid of dogs," I blurted out in one breath. "And I thought he really had his dog, so I freaked out and …"

"What do you want me to do?" Dad questioned.

"Tell him to stay off our block," I pleaded.

Dad looked at me. His patience drained as he shook his head disconcertingly. "I can't fight your battles for you," he lectured. "You are going to have to settle this by yourself." This was not a great time for my dad to teach me a life lesson, but I knew he was right.

I lowered my head and frustratingly kicked a stray stick off the deck as Dad waited for my response or a resolution to the problem.

He was right. I couldn't rely on others to fight my battles for me.

I sensed a grin growing on Jason's face behind me as I stalled for time. He thought he was in the clear.

"I guess you're right," I said to Dad, sounding dejected.

I immediately spun around, swung my closed fist at Jason's surprised face, and landed my first ever punch hard and square onto my defenseless target. I thought my fist was going to hurt from the sheer force of bone hitting bone, but I didn't feel a thing. Therefore, I punched Jason again, and again. I first punched him for making fun of my fear of dogs. I then found myself punching him for trying to affiliate himself with the my friends.

I took matters into my own hands and solved my problem.

But my dad lied. He got involved.

Dad was probably just as surprised as Jason by my sneak attack. He grabbed me away from my boxing bag and separated the two of us to opposite corners of the ring.

"Get in the house," Dad reprimanded. "Jason, you better go home."

I knew that I wasn't in trouble because I did exactly what my Dad told me to do. I stood up for myself. Jason's face looked like a science experiment gone terribly wrong. His blood combined with tears to create a demented painter's palette.

As Jason walked down the front porch steps, I noticed Jeff escaping into his house, hoping to go unnoticed.

◆   ◆   ◆

What is the significance of finding Jason on the side of the longest road I have ever driven on? I asked myself, as my earliest boxing contender entered the car. In death, it felt like everything I did and everybody I met induced some sort of puzzling meaning to my journey. I needed to confront them in order to continue.

I wondered if it was to remind me not to depend on others to justify my existence.

I killed my brother.

"I have to get him back."

"What did you say?" Jason asked.

"Huh? Oh, nothing," I replied.

"I can't believe you came for me," Jason brimmed.

"I can't believe you entered the shed on a bet," I responded.

"What shed?" Jason questioned, his brow furrowed in confusion.

Then it dawned on me. Maybe he didn't see a shed after all. Maybe I was the only person to have seen it all along. The shed was the home to my greatest fears. It was my hell. Mike and Jeff probably saw me enter something else in the middle of our cul-de-sac. Their hell. Whatever kept them up at night was what they cautioned me not to penetrate back home. How were they to know the evil lurking inside my grandmother's shed? I never told them about what happened in there. Likewise, Jason was probably dared to enter his version of hell, which again, was most likely not my grandparents' shed. It could have been a car, a building, or a swimming pool. How selfish of me to assume that everyone shared my fears. We all have our own hubs, or nuclei, unique to our persona and our demons.

We all see the same thing differently, I mused.

"What are you talking about?" Jason asked curiously.

"Never mind," I relented. It wasn't my business digging around in his subconscious analyzing the demons within, especially since I was having so much trouble navigating my own. I found it unfair that I was about to take him on a joyride through my own hell. But I desperately longed for the company.

I continued to drive down the same road as Jason reminisced. His thoughts spilled from his mouth like water out of a broken main. It was as if I was the can of oil freeing the Tin

Man's jaw, allowing Jason to share with me his meaningless reminders.

"Hey, where are you going?" the Tin Man asked.

"What do you mean?" I responded, my curiosity matching his concern pound for pound. *Can't he see that there is only one way to go.* The look on his face reminded me of the look after I clocked him with a right hook to the chin. *Did he know what was up ahead?*

"Where are you going?" he repeated, panic now gripping his voice. "Is this your idea of a sick joke?"

"I'm going to get my brother," I said calmly, not wanting to frighten him anymore than he already appeared to be. But my grip on the steering wheel tightened and my eyes locked onto the road ahead with unwavering certitude. He knew exactly what was up ahead, and it scared him … and me.

"Your brother is down there?" Jason sounded frightfully surprised. "You can't take me back. You won't."

I couldn't imagine how difficult his escape from hell must have been considering how difficult and taxing my descent was materializing into. I didn't know which feat was more formidable, but my destiny was beckoning me to forge forward. I was not about to turn around.

"Turn around," Jason ordered.

I wanted to tell him that I didn't risk my eternal afterlife just to rescue him. I had a much more important goal.

"I'm not leaving without Rob," I said. He sensed the car's acceleration forward and didn't know how to will my car into reverse. He was becoming frantic, searching desperately for something to hold us back.

"What's down there?" I questioned. "What will I find?"

Jason grabbed the steering wheel and jostled with me for control of the road.

Luckily, I had a lot of experience with people attempting to drive from the passenger's seat, from my father driving the golf cart to my brother driving my Cabriolet down the side of the highway to our eventual deaths.

Jason tried to pull the car off the road, and he was succeeding, as I started to lose my grip on the wheel. It's amazing how strong someone becomes when faced with imminent doom. *The fight or flight response.* I imagined my college psychology professor lecturing our class after watching a video of an old man lift a car to save his granddaughter.

I was wrong. Jason was no Tin Man guiding me down the newly paved yellow brick road. He was the Wicked Witch of the West steering me off-course.

Jason won our tug-of-war game on the steering wheel and he steered the screeching car off the road and into the cornfield. Jason let go of the wheel, and my out of control vehicle ripped through the cornstalks. I tried pumping the brakes, but the car didn't react.

More and more corn smashed into the windshield like a bug that had been flying dangerously low beside a busy highway.

All of a sudden I heard the jingle jangle of steel emanating from the backseat. I turned my head around to identify the noise, and there it was. My golf clubs were bouncing to the rhythm of my tumbling car. I turned back to Jason. We looked at each other in terror. I was reliving my death. The only difference now was that Jason replaced my brother in the scene.

One very determined cornstalk swung violently and cracked the windshield. Jason and I were now spiraling downhill. Realizing the outcome in a nightmarish déjà vu made dying again a lot harder the second time around.

As morbidly scripted, the front right wheel suddenly slammed into a rock jutting out of the ground, lifting the car into the air, and tossing it over as it smashed into a tree before falling back to earth, upside-down.

Glass and clubs were everywhere.

A deep gash ran against the grain of Jason's forehead, leaking blood all over his face and shirt. Once again, I didn't feel any pain. My stomach, however, was growling with eerily familiar severe aches.

Jason's glazed eyes turned to me as he whispered with all of his energy, "Help me." I reached over, grabbed his wrist, and held it tightly.

"I will, Rob," I said to him.

I knew I wasn't going to die because I was already dead. I wished that I could have died all over again because the pain in my stomach was unbearable, but the pain wasn't constant.

10

THE "A" WORD

My feet crashed into a double doorway as I lay on a bed with wheels. Masked men hovered over me and spoke in an indistinguishable tongue. One of them kept flashing a light pen in my eyes and writing notes into a small notepad as another hooked bags of fluids up to plastic tubes.

My stomach was reeling with the worst pain of my life, and I was strapped down, defenseless.

The men pushed me down a cold, dark hallway, their indiscernible jargon bouncing wildly off the stucco-brick walls. I watched the ceiling lights pass over me like heaven's windows allowing a glimpse, a tease.

I was experiencing the most displeasing case of déjà vu. However, I was in too much pain to try connecting the dots. Besides, it felt like everything was happening with the fast forward button taped down.

"You're such a brave boy," someone said to me. "We're almost there."

I puked clear liquid onto my moving bed, which was immediately wiped away. We pushed another pair of doors open, and we suddenly stopped.

One of the strangers, appearing out of focus, leaned over, felt my forehead, and snapped off his mask to reveal his worried countenance. He was a doctor. I smelled his antiseptic cologne from underneath his rubber gloves.

"You are going to feel a little prick," the doctor told me. "Then I want you to count to twenty. You'll be asleep before you know it."

What are they doing? I thought. *Why are they putting me to sleep?*

The sharp stomach pains augmented. Something told me, deep within the pit of my abdomen, that I wasn't on a bed with wheels for the accident Jason caused in my Cabriolet. I was being wheeled into an emergency room by a team of doctors for something much worse.

The head doctor, from what I could assess in my drugged-up stupor, pricked me in my bruised arm with a terrifyingly long needle, which could have easily come from the Loony Toons' props department.

"One, two, three, four," I counted aloud. The subsidiary doctors surrounded my bedside with all sorts of complicated machines, which they then attached to my fingers to better record my unique soul and convert the findings into a quantitative data analysis for inequitable comparison and judgment. As if two different souls could actually be analogized and universalized.

I didn't know what type of serum the doctors injected into me, however, as I counted myself to assisted sleep, I began to realize why I was about to go in for compulsory surgery ... for a second time.

"Is it the 'A' word?" I cried out. "The 'A' word?"

"Be quiet and keep counting," the head doctor warned.

"They said it wasn't the 'A' word," I continued. "They promised me that it wasn't the 'A' word. Let me go. I want to go home."

I was reliving a nightmare to painstaking accuracy and I was helpless to its voluminous call. I was told, a long time ago, that I would never have to experience such a virulent nightmare ever again. I packed a lifetime's worth of turbulence and heartache into three long weeks, rolling the dice on my future, beating the odds, and coming out on top, with the promise that the worst was over. And, here I was, going around in circles, back at the same craps table praying for a seven or eleven, but expecting the snake eyes. Not the best way to play the game.

I was lied to, and this time, there was no way out, so I continued counting my way to the twenty-second mark, all the while thinking that I wasn't supposed to have this. The pain wasn't constant.

"Five, six, seven, eight ..."

◆   ◆   ◆

"Is the pain constant?" I heard Dr. McMillan, my pediatrician, ask my dad impatiently through the phone's earpiece, as I squirmed in bed clutching my stomach in pain. He probably wasn't too thrilled about being awoken at 3:30 in the morning by a patient he already diagnosed as having a bad case of the stomach virus.

"Did you tell him that he has a 105 degree fever?" my Mom cried out nervously, as she held bags of ice on my forehead. "He looks green, goddamn it!"

I reached for the bowl of digested food, rare bodily fluids, and failed prescription medicine, and was looking forward to making another refund into the disgusting mix; a mix that even the most daring producers at *Fear Factor* would have to decline for competition. I had better nights.

"Is the pain constant?" my dad forwarded Dr. McMillan's question to me.

The pain wasn't constant. I would have the worst piercing sensation of my life, which felt like somebody was tearing my insides apart with a knife, and five minutes later, the pain would go away.

"If the pain isn't constant, then it can't be the 'A' word," I heard Dr. McMillan tell my Dad, sounding rather tired and perturbed. Even though I was only eleven, I was still old enough to figure out what the 'A' word stood for.

My doctor was either afraid to say the word appendicitis or he was so sure of his diagnosis that he wouldn't denigrate himself to making such fantastic claims out loud. After all, he had over a week to study my symptoms. How dare the parents of a sick child, who have no medical training whatsoever, question his livelihood? I stayed up the rest of the night, surviving on the whim of a doctor's telephone prognosis, completely unaware that in the morning, I would be strapped to a gurney at a hospital for emergency surgery to take out my ruptured appendix.

The surgery lasted nine hours, but the team of surgeons considered my status hopeless from the moment they opened me up and saw what was inside. Instead of getting their hands a little dirty cleaning a week's worth of puss out of my decaying body, they instead made a small incision, took out what was left of my burst appendix, sewed me back up, and called it a day. The doctors left the poison in me to continue covertly eating away at my insides.

There were a lot of dangerous bumps and hurdles on the road to recovery. Not only was I having difficulty eating, sleeping, and moving about, I was also having trouble doing things that I thought I knew by heart, like breathing, but nothing compared to my first CAT scan experience. The actual CAT scan of taking a picture of my stomach wasn't bad, but getting ready for the unusual photo shoot was a tremendously humbling night. I had to drink two bottles of a horrible white chunky liquid that resembled ground-up chalk the night before the CAT scan.

I was petrified to drink the doctor's concoction.

I was notorious for being a picky eater. My diet up through college consisted mainly of pizza, steak, bagels, and peanut butter and I would wash my bland food down with water, Sprite, or iced tea. For the most part, that was it. Friends would tease me for never trying a stick of gum, and Uncle Ricky would constantly beg me to expand my dietary horizons, but I was both stubborn and scared to treat my palate to something new. Therefore, I wasn't about to start exploring the wonderful world of culinary arts with two bottles of chalk milk. At least not without a fight.

"What if I can't, won't, or don't drink it?" I defied.

"Well, we'll have to insert a tube down your nose, into your stomach, and pump the liquid into you that way," Dr. Menon warned, trying to paint a gloomy scene.

"I'll take the nose tube," I requested.

Dr. Menon and the nurses immediately denied my request. They said that nobody had ever asked for the nose tube before, and that I would have regretted my decision.

I loved my family. I really did. Both my parents were with me for every second of my hospital stay, inspiring me to pull through and survive my hellish experience, however during the night that I was supposed to be prepping for my CAT scan, we said some very angry things to each other, all of which we didn't mean.

We, notice I said we, sipped, yelled, begged, and forced down as much disgusting liquefied chalk as we possibly could handle in five hours of torture. My dad insistently ordered me to grow up as I cried through my maiden voyage into the first pitcher of CAT scan juice. I took his remarks personally at the time, and was extremely vocal for a sick boy with my retributive hurtful words. However, in retrospect, I understood that we both just had enough, wanted all of this to be over, and to go home.

The results from the CAT scan revealed the surgeons' indolence for cleaning my insides out when they had the chance. The puss had almost completely consumed my body, the poison reaching dangerous levels. They called it peritonitis. I called it dirt. Dr. Menon explained to me, as if I brought this unfortunate situation entirely onto myself, that he intended to perform a second surgery to clean me out, but the only way he could do it successfully was to make a long incision down my chest, running from my neck down to my lower abdomen.

After the doctor left, I squeezed my parents' hands as tight as a fifty-pound child could, who weighed more from puss pockets than fat or muscle. I tried to hold back the tears because I was already dehydrated from my continuous upchucking, and I wanted to conserve my watery discharges. My skin had already become desiccated and flaky from the ban on water the doctors placed on me.

"We're going to do whatever it takes to make you better," Mom said. "If that means switching hospitals and finding a better doctor, then that's what we'll do."

"We're going to get you the best hospital in the country," Dad interjected, completely disposing of the superficial nasty comments he directed at me during the CAT scan incident. "All we want is for you to get better."

"What if the best hospital in the country is in California?" I asked.

"Then we're going to California," Dad replied immediately.

My parents were teaching me another lesson in the importance of family. They were sacrificing everything that they had to selflessly stand guard at the gates of my living nightmare to comfort and protect me from prospective danger, because simply that's what family is supposed to do, and not out of obligation or pity, but out of unconditional love. It is unconditional love that illuminates the darkened path, but it is our collective heartbeats that leads us to the light.

Even my brother, who was too young to visit the hospital, would shed more light onto my suffocating darkness by calling every night to urge me back to health. My seven-year-old brother, who I missed greatly, was genuinely there for me, as he always was and continued to be through the years. He wanted to tell the hospital that he was fourteen-years-old and short so he would be able to visit. I wondered whether I was capable of returning the favor so unreservedly.

Maybe I deserve this appendicitis after all.

Dr. Menon returned, holding the x-rays of my CAT scan high above his head, as if it were a fiery scythe, and approached me coldly. As I hid under my bed sheets, I imagined a tail would soon maturate from the enraged doctor before he'd effectuate a world of fire to my room. He grabbed my arm, which had already been badly bruised by his needle-happy nurses, and pulled me closer to him. He was hurting me badly.

"You're coming with me," Dr. Menon ordered.

All I could picture, as he urged me closer to him, was the unsettling image of Dr. Menon cutting my chest open from the neck down. I began to cry, and I once again prayed for my dad's help.

"Hey, get your hands off of my son," Dad said, as he doused the fire in the monster's eyes. Dr. Menon let go of me and blushed.

Dad returned the favor and grabbed Dr. Menon's wrist. I was suddenly safe again, as I felt another case of déjà vu infect me. "No more games," Dad commanded. "If this was your child, what would you do?"

Dr. Menon exhaled uneasily, like a fish on the sand unable to hold its breath any longer, and lowered his head. "I'd take him to another hospital," he quivered. He was beaten and exposed, the monster extinguished.

Although I was grateful, I thought, *it should have been my hand grabbing Dr. Menon's wrist.*

I remembered seeing my old baseball coach, a couple of my parents' friends, and my uncle. The next thing I knew, I was strapped and loaded into the back of an ambulance headed for Columbia Presbyterian. I pretended that I was on the back of a golf cart riding up the eighteenth fairway of Rockland Country Club. And, in a way, I was. Home free. Safe. The lights were blazing and the sirens were blaring as the ambulance reached ninety on the thruway as police escorted me all the way down to the hospital where Dr. Schwartz would save my life.

Along the way, as I battled my inner demons, disguised as peritonitis, I comprehended that my self-imposed limits were limitless, my antagonizing fears were cowardly, and my stifling loneliness was infinitely crowded with enriching love and begirding acceptance. I didn't reach my destination until I understood that there was no destination to reach after all, as long as I had loved ones nearby.

More importantly, I also rediscovered myself amongst a sea of doubt, figured out what I was made of in the face of asperity, and subscribed to my selfhood with unrelenting pride when I needed it the most.

I became the person that I always wanted to be on the three-month road trip back home from the hospital. Secure, balanced, confident, and comfortable. I wasn't a patient for a burst appendix. My pediatrician was right all along. In the end, it wasn't the 'A word' that caused me great pain and hardship.

I was hospitalized so I could go on an identity quest, which I thought that I succeeded in doing, until I once again found myself on my back in death, counting down the seconds until unconsciousness for yet another operation to remove my puss, or my inner demons, from my tainted body.

◆   ◆   ◆

"Eighteen … nineteen … twenty," I counted, not feeling tired at all.

"He's out," the head surgeon yelled out to his co-workers, as they all scampered about, some recording my heart rate and wheeling in expensive machinery, while others were busy sanitizing a box of sharp tools. "Let's get started."

"No!" I screamed. "I'm still awake!"

Nobody heard me.

"Scalpel," the head surgeon ordered. He held his hand out, which was protected by a rubber glove, and waited impatiently for one of his nurses to come by with the appropriate instrument.

"Wait!" I continued to scream. "The anesthesia isn't working. Don't cut me open yet!" I tried to generate tears to signal my consciousness, but nothing discharged.

"You're always ordering me around," I heard an approaching nurse cry out to the head surgeon as she handed him a long sharp razorblade and a needle.

"Don't start with me again," the head surgeon sighed, as he closely examined the pointy end of the needle in wonderment.

I tried to shift my position, but I was either strapped down tightly by protective shackles or completely paralyzed from the neck down by the anesthesia. Either way, I was defenseless to the forthcoming assault.

"Please stop!" I shrieked, almost tearing my vocal chords apart. "I'm not under!"

How could they not hear me? I wondered.

"You always do this to me," the nurse refuted. "Just because you're chief surgeon, it doesn't mean you can order me around … and that goes for in the bedroom too." At this time, the other doctors and nurses gathered around me, also unable to recognize my struggle to get their attention.

"See, this is why inter-office romances never work," one of the supporting doctors wisecracked, causing an uproarious scene of laughter.

I couldn't understand what was so funny. I was about to be cut open for a surgical procedure to remove poisonous puss while I was still awake, and my doctors were taking the whole thing very lightly.

"All right, let's get started," the head surgeon said, finally getting down to business. He proceeded to poke me with the long needle in my lower abdomen, which felt like a surprising punch in the gut. Luckily, the only thing that the needle extracted from me was my breath, but it still was painful.

If a little prick hurt me, I was afraid to experience the enduring sensations that would follow from making the incision with the recently sterilized knife.

"I found the spot," he continued. "Give me the knife."

"Please," I cried out. This was probably the most terrified I had ever been. I wasn't so sure anymore if my lips were moving when I spoke.

"Did you hear something?" one of the nurses said.

Hope!

Then there was silence. The masked men and women leaned over me, their heads forming an umbrella of malpractice, and stared at my emotionless face with a curious eye. A few beats of quietude passed as the doctors leaned in a little closer to my unresponsive body. My only response was an elevated heart rate causing a nearby machine to beep faster, which I surmised was normal considering I was cognizant of being cut open. I was screaming, but there weren't any external devices to translate my cries for the sterile doctors to hear.

"I guess I was just imagining things," the nurse said.

"Scalpel," the head surgeon barked.

"No!" I screamed. "Stop the operation." I thought that maybe if I counted to twenty again, I would fall asleep. "One ... two ... three ..."

I stopped counting because something cold, which felt freakishly refreshing, rested upon my stomach. It tickled me, and I wanted to laugh, but I knew it was the knife, and I feared that the next sensation the sharp razor generated wouldn't be so playfully invigorating.

My fears were confirmed when the knife pierced through every layer of my skin, tearing my microscopic pores apart to form an abysmal riverbed stretching across my lower abdomen, which rapidly filled up with my own blood. The pain was excruciating, and all I could hope for was to pass out from the traumatic experience.

"I need some towels!" the head surgeon yelled.

I tried to scream, sit up, do anything to signal my surrender, but I couldn't get the attention of my attackers. The head surgeon now had a clamp in his hand, which he used to spread my incision apart so far that I was almost turned inside out. Amazingly, my skin stretched like a rubber band. My entire insides were exposed for the doctors to play with and dissect … and I would be awake for the whole thing.

I never thought that I would ever experience pain like this. I always figured that there was a threshold to the amount of pain that people could endure. Anesthesia awareness shattered all presupposed thresholds.

"Kidneys, liver, prostate, bladder," the head surgeon chanted. He was naming all of my organs, sort of like a checklist prior to beginning.

I counteracted his naming of my organs by counting and praying. "Four … five … six … seven."

"He's got enough puss in him to kill five kids," I overheard one doctor say to another. On that note, all of them reached into my stomach with their hands and began scooping the puss out onto the floor.

"Eight … nine … ten …"

Puss and blood splashed across the head surgeon's mask, as he continued to extract my inner demons. I winced, unable to take it much longer, and tried to make myself noticed one last time.

"Ahhhhhh!" I shouted, as I felt a finger touch my pancreas.

11

BESIDE MYSELF

"Mom?" I asked. "Is that you?"

As I emerged from a deep drug-induced sleep, I rubbed my eyes to dissipate the blurriness in my vision so I could better assess my situation.

"We almost lost you, sweetie," Mom whispered, as she caressed my hair.

I was laying on an elevated hospital bed with a morphine button in one hand, and a television remote in the other. A Power Rangers episode aired on the TV set mounted on the far wall. *Just my luck,* I groaned. I didn't know whether to use the remote or the morphine to extinguish the annoying Power Rangers. Both would have worked just fine. I wondered how Rob could have ever liked that show.

I picked at my chapped lips, rolled up the extracted dry skin into little balls, and hid them under my fingernails.

"Thank God you're here," I exclaimed.

"No," Mom replied, smiling away tears of joy, "thank God *you're* here."

I rubbed my stomach gently and felt a track of staples sealing my freshly cut incision, which brought forth images of my doctor slicing my abdomen apart like a smoked sturgeon.

The nightmare is over, I boasted. *I survived the operation.*

Three tubes jutted out of my heart, through my chest, and into a rolling tree of medicated-filled IV bags. My new shadow, a companion, which would be with me for a long time. "I've got to get out of here," I told mom. "I need to rescue Rob."

"Don't be silly," Mom chuckled. "You're not going anywhere. You just had major surgery. Besides, Rob's gone."

Rob's gone? How could she …

"I've traveled so far!" I shouted. "You can't hold me back now."

"Yes, you've spiraled down a dangerous road," Mom replied. "A road that I warned you not to travel, but I'm not going to let you get back on. You've been saved. More than once. You're a lucky boy." She continued to stroke my hair.

Dr. Schwartz entered the hospital room wearing a stethoscope over his lucky New York Rangers' Mark Messier hockey jersey.

My savior, I cried, as the hairs on the back of my neck gave my childhood surgeon a standing ovation.

I was glad to see him after all of these years, especially in the uniform that brought our favorite hockey team the Stanley Cup while I recovered under his medical supervision for the side effects of an ill-treated burst appendix.

"How are you feeling?" he asked me in his most congenial tone.

"He thinks he can just get up and leave," my mother snorted, hoping for the doctor's support. *Here we go again,* I feared. *They're going to trap me here, and I'll never be able to get to my brother.*

"Where are you in such a hurry to go?" Dr. Schwartz asked. "You just woke up from surgery where I scooped out enough puss ..."

"... to cure five kids," I finished his sentence.

"Yeah, how'd you know?" he questioned.

"He thinks he can leave the hospital," my mother continued through nervous chuckles. She was doing everything she could to keep me hospitalized.

I had to keep reminding myself not to forget about my journey. I was not going to allow my mother, my doctor, or my IV leash hold me back.

Rob needed help. I was his only hope.

"Doctor, tell him he can't go anywhere," Mom requested, looking for support.

Don't get angry at her, I told myself. I realized that she was just another clever disguise of a tangent.

"Well, actually," Dr. Schwartz rebutted, "I'd encourage him to get out of bed and walk around the halls to build his muscles and stamina back up. And, of course, you'd have to be with him at all times to wheel the IV's and to make sure he's okay." He looked at me and winked. "Is that okay with you?" he asked me.

Is he on my side? I questioned. *Is he giving me an out?*

"Let's go for a walk now," I exclaimed, seizing my opportunity to escape. That was my first burst of energy since the operation … and it felt great.

"There's a game room on the fifth floor," Dr. Schwartz offered. "Take the elevator at the end of the hall." He checked the fluids in my IV bags, scribbled onto my chart, and smiled. "You're on the road to recovery. Stay the course and you'll be fine."

If only he knew what kind of road I took to get here.

"Let's take that walk," Mom relented.

◆   ◆   ◆

As I shuffled my feet down the desolate wing of the children's intensive care unit with my mother dragging the IV rack beside me, I thought I would try again to make my mother understand.

"I must look for Rob," I stated, hoping this time for approval as we waited for the elevator to arrive.

"It's too dangerous," she warned, tired of continuously rehashing the same argument. "You're trying to live in two worlds at the same time, and what you are going to find out is that what's important is where you are today, right now. You can't change the past or alter the future. It's all about right now. If you keep your delusion alive, you are going to forever end up in the limbo you are finding yourself in."

I had never heard my mother talk like that, and it made me a little scared. "We are going to stay here as long as it takes to make you better, and then I'm bringing you home," Mom concluded.

Ding!

The elevator doors opened. I stepped inside and pressed the button for the fifth floor, but as I stood in the center of the elevator shaft waiting to be vaulted upward by a complicated pulley system, I noticed that something wasn't right. Something was missing.

Where's Mom?

The elevator began to shut.

I panicked because my heart was still attached to the IV bags in the hallway, and the connecting tubes were about to be clamped shut by the converging doors. I frantically pressed all of the buttons in the elevator and pounded on the closing doors as I cried for my mom to come to the rescue.

"Help!" I screamed. "I promise not to leave."

I was afraid that if the elevator doors pinched my lifeline, my heart would then be pulled out of my chest as my space would ascend.

As the doors were closing, I could see the IV rack, my shadow, staring back at me in the shrinking space between the kissing doors, relieved to have left me behind before I journeyed further into my darkest depths. However, before we said our goodbyes, it wanted my soul, which it had hooked, and was now reeling in.

"Mom," I pleaded. "Please come back."

Fear robbed my vision. I couldn't discern the buttons I was pressing any longer. Seconds felt like hours. I was hoping that one of them was designated for aborting the operation ... or probably more helpful, calling for help. Just then, the doors clamped shut, concealing my shadow, and constricting my IV tubes into an airtight knot.

The elevator hummed and began to rise with half of me inside, and the other half, the condemned half, was ripping my heart out. Half of me, in the caged cell, possessing my future, which I didn't know if I could survive, felt the tubes creating tension in my chest as they questioned my intent.

I watched the number for the next floor light up as the pressure in my chest reached a breaking point.

I prayed for my heart to repel its attackers.

Ding!

The elevator reached the second floor and … I was still in one piece. As I touched my chest in search for a wound, I felt my heart racing from within.

No more tubes protruded out of my breast. I escaped the nightmare. I slid to the floor and rested my head against the far wall of the elevator shaft as I thanked my lucky stars for surviving yet another close call.

The elevator doors spread open. A pair of shiny black shoes stepped into my low-lying line of vision. I saw my reflection within the gluttonously applied shoe polish. As I looked up to identify the suited owner of the extravagant galoshes, I was stunned into confused silence. Either he was wearing the same shoe polish on his face, which allowed me to continue seeing my reflection, or I was staring up at myself. Astonishingly, the latter was the case.

I stood up and inspected my double. I wished somebody could have asked me who I was standing next to because I could have wisely volleyed back, "That's me ... I'm beside myself," and meant it literally ... for the first time. It was eerie. I noticed every idiosyncrasy that I possessed standing beside myself for thirty seconds, which every mirror in the world did not have the foresight to project for me in my lifetime. *It is amazing how differently you picture yourself when it isn't really yourself.*

My double, who was completely unaware of my presence, repeatedly wiped beads of sweat from his forehead with the side of his shaking forearm while he moved about in short compact nervous circles. He also wiped his balmy hands on his black pinstriped Armani pants. Something was bothering him.

Something was bothering me.

I wanted to ask myself what the problem was. However, judging by how I appeared to be invisible to my counterpart, I also surmised that it would be equally impossible to get through to myself vocally as well.

I needed to find a way to get in touch with myself.

All of a sudden, the elevator doors closed and the shaft began to rise with both myself ... and myself inside. *Where am I taking me?* I wondered.

As we elevated upwards, I watched the different floor numbers light up, wondering what the lucky number would be.

... 12 ... 23 ... 42 ... 48 ... 56 ...

Where could we be going?

If my other half retained the answer to my question, then he did not look too happy about our impending destination. He grew more and more nervous with every successive floor that we rocketed past. His heavy breathing compounded with his absurdly fidgety behavior as our craft soared well past the half-century floor.

… 62 … 68 … 72 …

Ding!

As the elevator reached the 72nd floor and eased to a stop, I knew exactly where I was being taken. I stared at the circular light denoting the floor number until it switched off, wishing that the pulleys would snap, and we would freefall back down to the children's intensive care wing at Columbia Presbyterian.

Instead, the doors opened.

I watched my double very carefully, fearing that I finally knew what was making him so nervous about the 72nd floor. After all, I was he.

He made one last attempt at masking his anxiety behind a mandatory corporate dress code. He jostled his tie into place, rubbed his eyes, put on his work face, and stepped out of the elevator with purpose and fortitude; a far cry from the nervous paces he was making during lift-off.

I lagged behind as the two of us entered my office.

Ding!

The elevator doors shut behind us. No way back!

12

THE 72nd FLOOR

The office was in perfect order. As always. The space within the four walls of the 72nd floor was just as sterile as the hospital room where I was saved from appendicitis. However, there was never any saving being done here. This was the place where I spent most of my adult life trapped for eight hours a day, five days a week.

The room was separated into small cardboard cubicles to hide the peasant floor employees from view as associates pushed papers on executive chairs behind locked doors in air-conditioned suites. The economic divide never appeared any clearer.

The main floor would always remind me of a complicated maze with no real way out. The cubicles adjoined one another to form intricate patterns that even the greatest scientific minds would not be able to crack. An aerial view of the floor would have yielded all of the employees stuck within the many dead ends of the labyrinth, having given up trying to reclaim their cheese of life.

The managers were like mad scientists controlling an unjust experiment. They joyously watched their claustrophobic subjects squirm for freedom as they tauntingly waved the key of life in front of their faces from a safe, protective distance. They would also give the trapped souls false hope for freedom with shiny substitutes for a life, such as money, a fancy title, and stock options. However, they could never replace the full benefits a soul could ever achieve.

Little did the managers know that they were just as dead as their trapped test subjects yearning to breathe free. Even more so. The decomposition rate was slower behind the three-inch oak wood doors they hid behind, but just as devastating.

I was guilty of being on both sides of the coin. I hated the associates' fabricated world built upon lies and deceit when I was an expendable bottom feeder. I also hated the rat workers cluttering up the main floor while making the company look bad after I was promoted to one of the head honchos.

As I followed myself into the main floor of my office, I realized it wasn't the people I hated. It was the phoniness. It was the lifelessness. It was the space within. I wasn't happy with anybody as long as the unfiltered corporate air was tainting my lungs like nicotine-laced tobacco. I felt very uncomfortable back on the 72nd floor. I never liked my job. I always imagined something better for myself.

◆   ◆   ◆

My friend's uncle landed me the job. I was twenty-five at the time. I had chased my dream of becoming a screenwriter into a dead end for three years, and it was time to navigate an easier avenue toward the ultimate finish line of success.

To make the job at the Barrymore Financial Services on the 72nd floor appear more important than it really was, the job description on the application sounded complicated, but my work was very simple. The job description read:

Responsibilities include, but are not limited to:

Monthly closes for multiple entities
Account reconciliations and analyses
Providing ethical competitive intelligence
Maintaining procurement metrics
Helping with expediting, as well as transactions
Identifying and supporting procurement involvement in areas of spending not currently undertaken
Working closely with procurement team members throughout the company to leverage buying opportunities & standardize processes/methods, whenever required

I didn't even know what a procurement was, but I promised to always provide ethical competitive intelligence and it got me the job. All that I really did in my personalized cubicle was tirelessly plug numbers into a computer between surfing the Internet for sites not blocked by the company and intense games of Snood. Never once did I have to leverage buying opportunities while standardizing processes/methods. I did, however, post controversial comments on the Yankees' message boards all day.

After five long years of serving the main floor and setting a personal record in Snood, I was promoted to supervisor. My responsibilities were very much the same as before, but I now had the privilege of plugging bigger numbers into a more expensive computer from a more comfortable chair in my own personalized office. I also had the authority to hire and fire the underlings.

My first order of business in my new position was to hire my brother, who was still searching for himself amongst a plethora of part-time jobs since graduating Arizona State University. I thought that maybe hiring Rob would allow both of us to continue our cross-country trip together from the 72nd floor. Maybe we would finally find what we were searching for.

Everything started out okay. Rob took over my old position and seemed grateful for the opportunity. He even moved into the same cubicle that I once had when I was a subordinate. For years, he simply faded into the backdrop, complementing the dull lifeless office furniture while unaware of the hold that the labyrinth had. Like the coffeepot and the water cooler, he was the perfect employee.

Rob was fooled every month into thinking that he had a fulfilling life with every passing paycheck, just like everyone else working on the 72nd floor. However, it is hard to keep a caged bird submissive forever, and my brother began testing the labyrinth walls for weaknesses.

Rob was going stir crazy, wondering when he would escape the maze and be promoted to supervisor to work alongside me. I wanted to explain to him that it didn't get any better with a more extravagant title, but I was too guilty for already making him feel lifeless by granting him a no-outlet profession on the 72nd floor. I kept my mouth shut and hoped that his aspirations would soon dissipate along with mine.

We weren't smothered by stalks of corn during this particular leg of our trip, but we continued to find ourselves stalled in a dead end cul-de-sac, the cubicle walls slowly closing in on our dreams, while the gases of life poisoned our lungs. Not only did I take my own life, I also sacrificed my brother's as well.

I couldn't be sure if he felt as trapped as I did. He enjoyed making the money. We simply found ourselves on the bottom rung of two different ladders. His, the economic ladder, and mine, the ladder to nowhere.

One Thursday afternoon, my boss, Travis Dicks, a pudgy man who covertly painted his face with makeup and unduly slicked his short dark hair back with gel to draw attention away from his unusually large teeth, invited me into his office for a one-on-one meeting to discuss the numbers being processed into the company computers. Trevor Dicks didn't like anybody. I was certain he sat in his office all day wondering how he would be able to generate the same amount of revenue for the company without having to employ anybody. For whatever reason, he had a certain amount of respect for me. He didn't like me, I didn't like him, but he trusted my judgment and extended my responsibilities.

"I've been going over this quarter's numbers," Dicks grumbled, as he reviewed a short stack of papers on his desk in dissatisfaction.

Maybe the reason why he tolerated me over all of the other employees was because I knew how to handle him during times of crisis.

"Somebody's gonna have to be held accountable," Dicks continued, his temper gaining momentum like a landslide. He then crinkled his upper lip and massaged his gums in anger, exposing his horse-like teeth. That was his signature intimidation move, as if he were saying, "Don't mess with me, or I'll latch onto your leg with my oversized choppers and never let go."

Like everybody else who had experienced 'the move', I had to keep myself from exposing my own teeth in laughter or else he'd bite my head off in one clean menacing chomp. There were so many e-mails circulating the office poking fun at our boss's teeth. If he ever caught wind of them, then there would be a lot of unemployed jokesters wishing they still had Travis Dicks' dental plan.

"I'm going to have to make a statement," he fumed. "I won't stand for numbers like this." He pounded his fist on the stack of papers.

I wondered how much the tooth fairy would put under his pillow if I knocked his two front teeth out. *Two, maybe three thousand dollars. I heard she pays by the pound.*

"What do you have in mind?" I asked.

"I want you to fire a few of the level A's," Dicks concluded.

Level A was a fancy term for the floor employees.

"But, Mr. Dicks, why should …" I started.

"I don't care who it is," my boss interrupted. "It doesn't matter. How can I be taken seriously when my company churns out numbers like this?"

"How can I terminate people if they had nothing to do with the losses?" I prompted, hoping that Dicks didn't have rabies. "Shouldn't we investigate the reason for the losses before we jump to wrong conclusions?"

"Investigate?" Dicks barked, his fangs thirsty for blood. "Do you know how much time that will take?" Travis Dicks dropped the stack of papers into a nearby receptacle, stood up, and glared at me, his lip tired from massaging his chaffed gum. "We will act now. We'll take arbitrary termination to a new level. We'll do it publicly. This will show the others that nobody is safe. And then, I guarantee we'll never see another quarter like this again."

I understood completely. According to Dicks' plan, it really didn't matter who was fired. Their termination was a symbol. A sick and twisted message to the unlucky survivors of floor seventy-two, warning them to reverse last quarter's trend or else the same fate would befall them. It was exactly how my dad solved the bee infestation problem during the burning bush incident. He allowed a few of the yellow jackets to survive the blast so they could tell others not to make the same mistake twice. And we never had a bee problem again.

"Make your decisions by the end of today," Dicks lectured. "I don't care how you do it. Pick names out of a goddamn hat for all I care."

I sat in my office wondering how I could make this decision as easy as possible. I tried pulling names out of a hat, but I was never satisfied with my selections, promising myself that the next dive into my 1996 New York Yankees' World Series hat for a name on a crumpled piece of paper would be the official pick. It didn't work. I was unable to make an 'official' drawing. I even tried pulling everybody's file up on my computer and choosing the ones who had the most blemished records in aiding my decision, but nobody's file infamously stood out enough to help make a morally accurate resolution to my dilemma.

I was moments away from giving up. I wanted to march into Mr. Dicks' office and surrender my title. I wanted to tell him to fuck off and then jump out of his office window on the 72nd floor and do a face plant on the sidewalk. However, before I could do all of that, I found myself mesmerized by an old family Christmas photo of my brother and me playing in the snow. I stared at the two of us for what seemed like as long as we were frozen as children in the picture frame. And then suddenly, a disturbing realization came over me like an unshakable cold.

I found my target. I realized I could kill two birds with one stone. I could satisfy my boss' order and I could save my brother from this corporate hell.

My finger held down the intercom button as I leaned toward the phone's speaker. "Mary, if anybody comes looking for me …" I said, my voice wavering and pitch bending awkwardly. "Tell them I stepped outside for a moment to get some air."

I think I stood up, adjusted my suit, and walked out of my office. I couldn't be so sure anymore because, at that moment, I wasn't myself. I wasn't even the one who placed the phone call to my secretary.

Someone had claimed my body and was taking me to the elevator so we could inhale some fresh air together on the ground floor, seventy-two stories away from the suffocating stench of a fabricated uncomfortable lifestyle, before ascending back up to carry out a befouled assignment together.

I was beside myself.

I figured I was in for a wild ride, and I wouldn't be able to raise the safety bar and dismount until the roller coaster came to a complete stop.

"I found my target," my captor said through my lips.

◆   ◆   ◆

I never thought I would have to navigate the corporate maze of hell ever again after I died, but here I was, standing next to my nervous double on the 72nd floor about to pilot through the office cubicles in search of my brother.

"I don't want to go in there," I tried to explain to my other half.

He still couldn't hear me. I was beginning to realize that my double was also fighting the urge to stay out of the maze. However, a higher power was drawing him, us, me in. I took off my shoes to keep me grounded. The tiles felt as cold as death underneath my feet. It wasn't at all like frolicking barefoot in the grass and mud as a child. Seventy-two floors away from earth's epidermis. I was detached.

My double sucked in a giant supply of the room's decade old uncirculated air and immediately blew it back out dissatisfied before stepping into the maze.

I followed behind.

"We don't have to do this," I pleaded. "Let's call the whole thing off."

My double appeared driven. All nervousness had disappeared behind his mask of professionalism, a pre-requisite garment for visiting the 72nd floor.

"I'll pick out of a hat for real this time," I continued, practically impelled to tears as I tried to keep up with the double. "We're making a huge mistake."

He didn't even break stride. We were making turns through the maze like seasoned professionals, passing nothing but vacated cubicles along the way. Every workspace was like its own little habitat, specifically decorated for its unique endangered caged species to feel more at home.

I followed my double around one final turn, unable to talk him into backtracking. It was too late anyway. We were already deep within the complicated twists and turns of the labyrinth. We'd be lucky if we escaped at all.

As I had expected, he led us right into my brother's cubicle. The first thing I noticed was the very same Christmas photo that I had framed in my office resting beside a desk calendar. The second thing that I noticed took me by surprise.

"Rob," I said simultaneously with my double.

Rob, caught slightly off-guard by the sudden intrusion, curiously spun around in his chair, losing yet another stare-off with the computer screen, and then smiled upon identifying the perpetrator of the sneak attack.

"You startled me," he said. "Is it lunch time already?"

I found him. I couldn't believe my eyes. I had embarked on a most difficult journey to locate my brother in the most infamously dangerous place in death, and I conquered my own monsters along the way to travel deeper than anybody would ever admit to traveling. Everybody, including my father, said I wouldn't be able to do it. But here I was, on the precipice of bringing Rob back to Grandma's, hopefully in time for Christmas dinner, and I was still standing. I couldn't wait to see Grandma again. She was the only one who believed in me. She was the only one who wanted the dining room table to stretch to its limits once again.

"Let's get out of here," I exclaimed.

A look of concern flashed across Rob's face.

"What are you doing here?" he asked suspiciously.

"I've come to take you home," I said excitedly.

What's with him? I wondered. *Why isn't he thrilled to see me?*

"We need to talk," my other half rudely interjected during our reunion. "Should we do it here or over lunch?"

"What's wrong?" Rob replied, sensing the worst.

He doesn't even see me, I realized.

"Rob!" I screamed, flailing my arms wildly for his attention. "Over here … I've come to take you home."

"Can I sit?" my double asked Rob.

It was all one big tease. He didn't see or hear me no matter how ostentatious my efforts were to attract his attention.

I wasn't on the precipice of saving him, I realized.

I was probably lured further away from my destination, fooled into the cursed labyrinth, once again by the disguised siren's songs of temptation.

The devil knows how to put on a show with many costume changes. I wanted to know where my real brother was. More importantly, I wanted to know which half of me was the authentic half.

I should have known that it wasn't going to be that easy. For the first time, I was stuck inside a movie where nothing was real except for the illusions, mirages, and impostors before me. I had no chemistry with my supporting cast. They weren't delivering the correct lines of dialogue and they weren't following the proper set direction. I felt like a helpless prop pleading to be included in the scene.

What if everything around me is reality and I am the intruding impostor? Suddenly, my entire world was repeatedly shaken and flipped upside down like a forecasting magic eight ball providing none of the appropriate answers.

"Rob, am I getting through to you at all?" I asked impetuously. I had to cut this scene before it reached its unforgiving climax, having witnessed firsthand its repercussions. I had to stop my other half from once again making a fatal decision.

"The thing is … well … how should I put it?" my double uttered nervously to Rob. He was trying to peel away the Band-Aid softly, but I could tell that it was painful.

"Just come right out and say it," Rob replied sternly. He wanted the Band-Aid to be ripped off quickly so he could determine how deep the wound would be.

I was screaming my head off like an angry director trying to exercise control over his unruly hired hands. It was all a waste of energy though. I was not receptive to their senses. I wished that I, too, were deaf and blind so I wouldn't have to experience the forthcoming nightmare.

"We have to lay you off," I heard my double explain to Rob.

Rob's insides crumbled to the ground as he sat in his chair in stunned silence. It was hard for me to watch myself destroy my brother's life, but I was still trapped deep within the maze with nowhere to run or hide, and I was forced to observe ... again. I tried to stop myself from doing it, but I was too detached to comprehend my warning signs.

I was deaf and blind after all; I wasn't receptive to my own senses.

Nobody had claimed my body. I wasn't possessed or having an outer body experience. I didn't dichotomize.

I fired Rob, I realized. *It was my decision.*

It was time for me to start accepting the blame.

"Are you serious?" Rob asked my double, still shocked from the pain induced by the Band-Aid's tear. "Why? Is this your decision?" His voice was cold and trembling.

My double nodded, his nauseous brain coughing up perspiration through his forehead. His head was probably spinning uncontrollably, making his brain even dizzier than it already was because my double staggered momentarily as he turned away from Rob's watery eyes, having to clutch the desk to regain his balance.

"I'm sorry," my double choked.

Rob, deep in thought, lowered his head and rubbed his temples.

"The company is ..." my double started.

"Don't," Rob chimed in, as he placed his faulty magic eight ball in his quivering hands and wondered about his uncertain future.

"I'll tell you what," my double continued, his voice brimming with a hint of inappropriate energy and excitement. "We'll go golfing. Just you and me. There's a long weekend coming up. Let's go upstate and play on some really nice courses."

I turned pale. I didn't make the connection until I had the opportunity to witness myself fire Rob from a third person point of view.

"I killed my brother," I declared stoically.

There is nobody to blame but myself, I thought.

I killed my brother three days before I drove him into a tree. I killed Rob in the labyrinth.

I knew it was useless to try convincing my brother not to take me up on my invitation. He couldn't hear me. He died. I pulled the trigger well before my Cabriolet finished the job.

"I'm sorry," I cried. "I'm sorry."

No response. I had to free myself from this nightmare. I had to break away from my destructive double before he did anymore damage.

I rubbed my feet on the linoleum floor and ran through the labyrinth walls, knocking down the abutting cubicles like a world champion domino player. I locked my eyes on the large office window as I forged forward, zeroing in on my target. Normally, I would stand beside the window with a coffee in my hand admiring the high-rise view with innocuous suicidal thoughts. But now, I had seen enough. I couldn't go on anymore. I was giving up. I didn't know any other way to escape the never-ending road, so I jumped. I seamlessly penetrated the window like a marathon runner into a thin strip of finish line tape, glass shattering everywhere, and nose-dived seventy-two floors onto the surrounding blacktop.

13

THE HIMALAYAS

Uncle Ricky was right. It was a most wondrous sight. The snow-capped mountains of the Himalayas ripped through the drifting clouds and soared into thin cold air, grazing heaven's impermeable border. I shivered at its imposing stature and wondered how Uncle Ricky could have believed I could overcome such an obstacle.

I stood up and stared at the majestic barrier before me. I panned across the hazy horizon and strained my neck, attempting to reach the rocky jagged mountaintops rising for freedom much like the stalks of corn on the side of the highway.

Nature's skyscraper was probably just as deep as it was high. I shivered again, but now it was a result of the temperature. I seemed to have shivered back into the dead of winter. I saw my breath in the cold frosty air. In all of my years of winter experience, I sensed the imminence of snowfall, and I looked forward to being swept away in the drift, far away from the monster in front of me.

I tried to turn around and backtrack through the more merciful flat ground behind me, but a strong breeze slapped me in the face and choked my retreat. The wind was as strong and impenetrable as the mountain before me.

Most of the times, you do not create your own hurdles, I heard my uncle lecture.

I rubbed my exposed arms, wishing I were sitting by the fireplace in my grandfather's extension. I slowly walked up to the face of the mountain, feeling the weight of my conscience affected by the strong gravitational pull towards the most foreboding crest in the mountain range.

I knew where I had to go. The wind whipping against my back was nudging me closer to my greatest barrier. My starting point.

I looked down at my feet and noticed that I had left my shoes at the office.

I knew that if I ever wanted to sit around the Christmas pile on my favorite gray chair next to the cackling fireplace with my family again, then I would have to go through the freak of nature standing in my way.

"Baby steps," I told myself. I never climbed a mountain before, but I figured that the best way to ascend the impossible was to concentrate on each step; break the enterprise into a million individual goals. "Baby steps," I repeated.

The wind picked up as snowflakes danced toward my bare feet. The mountaintops must have punctured a hole in heaven's floor because the snowflakes looked like falling angels.

"Christmastime is here again," I said. I felt it in the air. I was so close to recapturing the long lost traditions that I so desperately desired. I caught glimpses of them in the melting snow angels and they were beautiful.

It was time to end my procrastination. I collected myself, took a deep breath, and stepped forward onto the mountain's substratum with my right foot.

"One goal complete," I said. "Now only about a billion steps to go."

My left foot followed my right's lead, and I suddenly found myself walking up the face of the mountain barefoot in the twilight of a blizzard. I marveled at the star-filled sky, anticipating a climb that would take me to the constellations where I could relax in both dippers, hold hands with Orion, and ride Pegasus into the night.

Uncle Ricky would be so proud, I thought. *I am finally hiking the Himalayas.*

As the sun set behind the mountainside, the glaciers glistened from the summit. More snowflakes made their way down from heaven, blanketing me an aura of confidence, with the warmth of tradition. The day's final rays of sunlight splashed across the evening landscape.

It was the second most ravishing snowfall I had ever been a part of.

◆   ◆   ◆

It was October 3, the last night at Uncle Ricky's summer home in Sagaponack. Rob and I were helping our uncle pack all of his belongings into his brand new 1987 white Cabriolet convertible before he had to return the beach house keys.

Uncle Ricky had rented the same beach house in the Hamptons for three consecutive summers, and in that time, he never had so many people claiming to be his friend seeking an invitation. It wasn't so much the house that attracted his guests. The house was deceptively dingy-looking on the outside, comprised of rotting wood concealed by peeling paint, however, the real reason why everyone flocked to Uncle Ricky's summer home was for the enchanting beachfront property hidden behind New York's expensive front door.

From the sand-coated back deck, a visitor would immediately be greeted by a cool ocean breeze and the soft ruffling sounds of rolling water. A slender wooden walkway would chauffeur one from the end of the deck through a thin trench of cottontails and sand dunes to the central stimuli. A short trek across the ramp, passing over the uninhabitable snake-infested marsh, would at last take the visitor into a private paradise, leaving behind the weight of the world to relax and get lost among an ocean of nature's beauty.

The ocean was always as clear and blue as the Hampton sky. The never-ending breaking waves slowly grounded the concomitant sand into a fine powder that gently massaged the soles of my tired feet as I floated effortlessly toward the all-forgiving, all-healing water. It was a perpetual attack on mankind's stained turf, and one day, millions of years from now, the ocean will wipe the slate clean of our sins.

"Once upon a time, you came from the ocean," my dad told me, as we stood together in paradise, the water receding under our feet.

"What do you mean?" I asked. I was nine years old and I interpreted everything literally. "You and mom found me in the ocean?"

"We all came from the ocean," Dad said, laughing at my naivety. "You ... me ... and even your brother. This is every-one's home."

For five months out of the year, Uncle Ricky was the key master. There were so many friends and family members look-ing for a way to escape the manufactured world and finally come home.

I did most of the packing by myself on that unseasonably brisk fall evening. My brother was too young to be of any help, and Uncle Ricky was busy filling out last-minute paper-work at the dining room table. There were quite a few boxes and shopping bags that needed to be squeezed into the Cabri-olet's tiny backseat, and I spent about an hour in the driveway fruitlessly trying to stuff everything into the limited space. Rob taunted my efforts each time I pulled Uncle Ricky's belongings out of the car to start all over again in search of a more efficient packing system.

"It's like cramming ten pounds of shit in a five-pound bag," he laughed. Both Rob and the new Cabriolet were getting on my nerves. I tried loading the car every which way, but I couldn't solve the puzzle without running out of storage.

◆   ◆   ◆

I wasn't as tactful as my dad who during every Christmas Eve morning, successfully packed his car to the brim with all of our Christmas gifts to be brought down to Grandma's. He usually succeeded on his first try, too. Dad did it so systematically that there was still enough room for Rob and I to fit in the backseat. It was our first way of gauging how big the Christmas pile was going to be that year. The more scrunched over and uncomfortable Rob and I had to sit on the car ride down, the taller the mountain of gifts would be when we awoke on Christmas Day. We loved having no room in the car. It was always best when my foot would fall asleep. On those rare occasions, Rob and I expected a record-breaking day for the family's oldest holiday tradition.

"How do you do it?" I would ask dad. "How do you fit everything in so easily?"

"Look how much space I have to work with," Dad claimed, as he wrapped a rope around the trunk of the car to keep the over packed gifts from spilling out during our trip. "I'll never run out of room in there."

I thought he was crazy, however, no matter how big we became, he still figured out a way to cram everything into the car's available space.

◆　　◆　　◆

"Uncle Ricky," I said, as I walked apprehensively into the beach house and up to my busy uncle. "I can't do it. I need your help."

He looked up from his paperwork and sighed. "What do you mean you can't do it? You're eleven years old. People your age are hiking the Himalayas."

"Your new car is too small," I rebutted.

"I'm sure you'll find a way," he responded, as his attention slowly returned to the small print on the paperwork before him. "Just be careful. Some packages are fragile."

I trudged back outside and returned to the Cabriolet for one last try. I picked up a large duffel bag filled with clothes and opened the driver's side door.

I reclined the driver's seat forward and attempted to shove the duffel bag into the backseat. I punched the bag in frustration and kicked the side of the car. I hated Uncle Ricky's new car.

"You can't do it, you can't do it," Rob teased, as he ran circles around the car.

I was about to sprint after Rob and teach him to keep his mouth shut, but then it dawned on me. "I have all the space in the world," I said, a smile sprouting through the cracks in my mouth. "All I have to do is unlock the limitless sky."

I unhooked the Cabriolet's roof and pulled the top down to introduce the car's confined interior to the infinite available space above it. It was so simple. I was now able to stack the packages any way I wanted to because of my newly employed star clogged ceiling. It took me no less than five minutes to fill the backseat with Uncle Ricky's belongings. I felt like my dad after he would successfully utilize the limitless space inside of his car to pack the family's gifts the morning before Christmas.

Rob joined me as we collectively admired my work of art in the gravel driveway of my uncle's soon-to-be former summer beach house. I couldn't take my eyes off of the Cabriolet. I loved it. After my adventure of packing and unpacking and packing again, I became a part of the vehicle. I knew almost every inch of it from tapping into all of the procurable hidden space. I forecasted that someday the car would be mine.

"Looks like you figured it out," I heard Uncle Ricky say, as he approached the car to give his stamp of approval. "I told you it was easy."

Uncle Ricky stood beside me and held out the key for the car.

"What's that?" I asked, knowing exactly what was dangling from his finger.

"Take it for a spin," he pushed. "For a job well done."

"But, Uncle Ricky, I'm only eleven years old."

Uncle Ricky jingled the key in front of my face. "Are you going to use that excuse for the rest of your life?" he asked disappointedly. "Come on, people your age ..."

"I know, I know," I moaned, grabbing the key from his outstretched finger. "People my age are hiking the Himalayas." I studied the key as it rested in the palm of my shaking hand.

"Can I come?" Rob shouted.

"Let's go," Uncle Ricky said, as he motioned for both of us to join him in the already crowded car. "To the end of the road and back."

It was like Christmas, but better. I drove the Cabriolet to a stop sign one hundred yards away as Uncle Ricky coached warily from the passenger's seat. I then attempted a K-turn, and brought the car back to the beach house in one piece. It was the greatest gift I could ever receive. My first experience behind the wheel proved to be a successful one, much more successful than my last.

"How'd it ride?" Uncle Ricky asked me, as we climbed out of the car.

"Like butter," I responded, tapping into my limited knowledge of driving.

"Come on," Uncle Ricky continued. "Let's go say goodbye to the ocean."

It was hard for Uncle Ricky to part with the beach house every summer, but this time around, he appeared to be more distressed than ever. He was unusually quiet. He would often stare off at nothing for an uncomfortable period of time in an obvious state of deep nostalgic reflection. He made a concerted effort to spend some time in each room of the house alone. I wondered whether he knew that this was going to be his last summer renting the place out.

He must have felt the same way when the family extension was demolished.

"It's nighttime," my little brother said. "Did you turn the beach off?"

I playfully punched Rob in the arm as we slowly made our way out to the beach.

We sat on the sand and watched the water flirt with our feet.

"I was born in the ocean," I said to Uncle Ricky, repeating my father's claim.

"Are you a fish?" Rob teased.

Uncle Ricky was silent. His eyes were stretching out to sea. I followed his lead so as not to disturb the moment. Only the waves were talking.

Paradise.

And then it began to flurry. October snow tumbled gently down from the sky to mingle with the ocean. "It's snowing," Uncle Ricky delighted.

It was one of the most beautiful sights in the world. Summer and winter had become one indistinguishable season that night.

"It's Christmas," Rob shouted, as he caught snowflakes with his tongue.

It was Christmas, and I was responsible for making it come early by packing Uncle Ricky's car like my dad had exhibited so many times before on the eve of the family's most coveted tradition.

We continued to sit in paradise amongst a most bizarre snowstorm while saying our final goodbyes to the ocean, our home.

◆   ◆   ◆

I continued to climb, fighting exhaustion, frostbite, and fear. The once captivating snowfall had quickly turned deadly and impassable. If it was true that everything originated from the ocean, then I was drawing further away from home the more I scaled the dangerous Himalayan path.

All of my mindless hiking made me lose track of time. I assumed it was nighttime. Usually darkness was a dead give-away to the realization of night, but I also considered that my elevation was so high that I had possibly escaped the reach of the sun's blanket of light and climbed my way up to everlasting twilight.

My visibility neared zero as I trudged higher and higher with my feet doing a great impersonation of purple blocks of ice. The winds were whipping the blinding snow into my face, freezing my nose hairs, which were making it extra difficult to breathe, compounding the already burning sensation in my lungs, effectuated by the perilous thinning air. Every time I inhaled, I feared I would burn a hole in my aggravated air sockets and fall back down the mountain. Death by frozen nose hair suffocation. Death by jagged rock colliding against unprotected head.

But I was already dead. The element of fear should have been eradicated from the calamitous equation. However, there was a mysterious constant affecting the solution to the word problem that caused me great uneasiness about my already determined fate. The physical and mental strain forced upon me by nature's largest pimple made me wish that I was still alive so I could perish once again to stop my misery. Looking forward to death was not a viable option anymore. Death was not my escape from the Himalayas' pestilential incline.

I was stuck.

My only hope of survival, for the sake of my physical and mental duress, was stumbling upon change, any type of change, during my eventual descent down the opposite side of the mountain.

"I hate Rob." I shivered, as I continued to fight gravity with two numb feet and ten useless toes, powerless to run wee wee wee all the way home. He was the reason why I was stuck inside the dark clouds cloaking the inspiring nighttime stars from sight. He was the reason why I was left clinging onto the planet's last wall of defense waiting helplessly for the opportune time to leap into the infinite sky for my maiden ride on Pegasus through the Milky Way.

Baby steps, I coached myself.

"Who am I to change people's fate?" I asked myself. "Rob killed Mr. Henderson. He belongs on the other side of this mountain. He deserves everything that he's got coming to him. The judge's verdict is irreversible because it is never wrong."

Easy does it, I warned. *You can't quit now. Just remember to take baby steps.*

"Rob!" I screamed, as I momentarily collapsed on my back and into a pile of packing snow. "You are now killing me! I hope you're happy."

I flapped my arms and legs in the snow to form a snow angel as I cried for freedom, but my tears were immediately frozen into place by the blistering cold. I wished that I would become buried in the falling snow, locked away forever, so I would never have to be afraid again. I knew it wasn't going to be that easy though. There was only one way out.

I can't believe I said that about my brother, I reflected.

"It's all his fault," I barked.

I was beside myself again, arguing bootlessly with my counterpart on the crest of the Himalayan summit while we made snow angels together like children, more specifically, like Rob and I as children, enjoying an unexpected snow day off from school underneath the street lamp and on top of a mound of newly plowed snow.

"I'm sorry, Rob," I muttered, as I closed my eyes and waited impatiently to be buried in the collecting precipitation. Me, my pessimistic counterpart, and the angels impressed into the snow, lay face down into the mountainside.

I'm sorry.

14

BAPTISM IN THE SNOW

"No!" I screamed, as I pulled myself up from the heavy snow, feeling refreshed and determined for the first time since stepping on Everest. "You will not beat me."

I stood up and glared at the mountain, no longer cold. No longer scared.

"I am not afraid," I said.

I took one giant step up the mountain, followed by another.

And another.

The blood had returned to my feet, allowing me to grip the rocks easier with my toes as I climbed. I was ascending the hazardous barrier at a marathon runner's pace and I smelled the glacier-covered summit growing stronger with every step.

So much for baby steps, I concluded. I had to make up for lost time. Rob was waiting for me on the other side of the mountain and I had to apologize for momentarily giving up on him.

The visibility had improved greatly since my rejuvenation in the snow, and for the first time, I was able to enjoy the

Himalayan scenery that Uncle Ricky had always wished for me to experience ... for the both of us.

I thankfully reached a short plateau, giving my tired feet a momentary break from scaling scabrous icy rocks. I floated across a colorful poppy field as the falling snow regressed to a light flurry.

A lull in the storm? I wondered.

The thick high grass grabbed at my knees, as if they were trying to hold me back from advancing forward, but I continued to quicken my pace toward an even steeper incline up ahead without becoming entangled by their malicious blades. The rich green field and the comprising extravagant flora were eerily reminiscent of the poison laced poppy field protecting the Emerald City.

I made it across in record time, and in one piece, with one more leg of the trip to go before reaching the top of the mountain. Deciduous Christmas trees dotted Everest's final incline. Beautiful layer cake waterfalls emptied the unlocked summit glacier water into a dynamic river, which ran down the forestry mountainside and discharged into the radiant green plateau to feed the fertile field of plant life soil with the necessary nutrients to sustain life in a treacherous environment.

I wondered how life could exist at an altitude where the air is thinner than a slice of college-ruled paper, but I was too determined at the task at hand to start hypothesizing and conducting environmental tests on Mother Nature's vacillating laws of the land. I noticed an old decrepit shack nestled by a patch of purple flowers in the distance, which further confirmed this atmosphere's ability to sustain life. The shack appeared to be abandoned and unkempt for years, which also suggested this paper-thin air's potential for serious paper cuts. I couldn't take my eyes off the shack as I continued to cross the plateau.

"Where have I seen this before?" I asked myself. For some reason, I was deeply attracted to the deserted house, which was probably home to an adventurous local looking for the ultimate solitude. It was reeling me in like a polar bear to a fish. I had to keep myself from being drawn off-track again.

"Come here, boy, and help me count down to lift-off," I heard a voice snarl.

"Mr. Henderson!" I shouted, as I quickened my pace. I didn't know whether I imagined his voice or actually heard it. I didn't want to find out.

The mountain shack reminded me of my grandparents' shed. I didn't have anymore time to soak in the scenery. I would have loved to sit by the rolling river and admire the foam build up against the banks where the weathered rocks glistened under the crystal-clear water, but I had an unbreakable date with the summit, and change awaited me on the other side.

"I am not afraid," I chanted. "I am not afraid."

I'll sightsee next time, I promised myself. *I'll take Uncle Ricky.*

I reached the inside of the clouds. I couldn't calculate how much climbing it took to get there. It felt like either five minutes or five months. The attenuated air must have affected my concept of time.

I remembered laying on my back as a kid with my brother describing and naming the passing clouds, wishing I could jump into the sky and float on top of the self-appointed animal-shaped concentrated moisture. Now I was there, not floating, but trying to escape the sky's teary eyes by climbing further up the mountain, high above the dark rain clouds of my own subconscious. A dense fog engulfed the slope, once again impairing my visibility. I used my sense of smell to find the icy cap. The aroma was overwhelmingly invigorating. As I inhaled their beauty into my system, I felt the holes in my lungs repair. Now I just needed something to fix the painful hole in my heart.

My plan was to shed all of my impostor layers away until all that was left was a fearless guilt-free child with his head above the clouds and the weight of the world under his feet.

Uncle Ricky would always tell me stories of an air so pure that it cleansed the soul of all of your self-doubts and self-assessments. I imagined that this was what I was experiencing, as I collapsed face first into the summit snow.

I finally reached the top of the mountain. I wasn't too tired to enjoy my unbelievable accomplishment, but I had to keep telling myself that my journey across the Himalayas was only half over. What goes up must come down.

I was surrounded by ice and snow on Everest's summit, which I presumed had never melted since the beginning of time. I could have been on the boreal deserts of Antarctica or the North Pole for all I knew, but instead, I was standing on the highest point that earth had to offer to its most audacious inhabitants. Even though the ice and snow had never changed its state in years, the infrequent passerby would most definitely experience a new humbling outlook on life while trekking through the collection of 10 million year old snowflakes and icicles.

I tried to look down and locate my starting point, but the peaks to the other mountains in the Himalayan range were blocking my already obstructed view of the ground. No matter which way I turned, all that I saw for miles were much shorter peaks blanketing the surrounding flat ground.

"It's all downhill from here," I told myself.

I tried to psyche myself up as I prepared to descend Everest's rocky backside. Before I could continue my voyage, something on the summit caught my eye.

An object was partially sticking out of the snow approximately fifty yards from me. *I haven't seen this before.* Curiosity momentarily defeated my sense of urgency, and I made my way over to the mysterious object.

"A Christmas gift," I delighted. A box with a ribbon wrapped in red patterned Santa Claus Christmas paper poked out of the snow.

Could it have been one of the presents that Dad packed in the cramped car. If so, then the infinite sky is truly the limit for the family tradition.

I knelt down beside the box and read the label aloud. "To Rob …"

I looked for another name.

Who could be giving my brother a gift?

There was no name on the label denoting whom the gift was from.

I wonder what's inside.

I was about to apply my skills of guessing the inclusive gift from the shape, size, and weight of the box, but when I pulled the present out of the snow, my attention was immediately shifted elsewhere as the mountain began to rumble under my feet.

"Earthquake!" I screamed.

The mountain was trembling so violently that I thought it was going to crumble. I tried to maintain a standing position on the snowy summit, but I couldn't stay vertical.

The 10 million year old stagnant snow started sliding down the mountain, as if the imprisoned flaky deposits were trying to make up for lost time, and I was fighting with all of my might not to let them take me for a ride. I struggled onto a nearby rock and hoped that the disturbance would pass. Mount Everest was alive, and I feared that I might have just awoken a sleeping giant.

Just then, a small crack materialized in the rock directly between my feet, and as the mountain's stentorian tremors increased in intensity, the small crack snaked across the mountain face at a rapid rate. The rift ran deep, and it was only a matter of seconds before the entire rock broke apart with me on top of it.

I clutched Rob's mysterious Christmas gift and dashed down the mountainside, trying to stay ahead of the oncoming avalanche. I ran barefoot, wishing that I had my boogie board to surf down the mountain, hoping that I didn't lose my footing, as I imagined breaking waves on my board in Sagaponack. No matter how fast I ran, I couldn't seem to put any distance between a possible fatal natural disaster and myself. A tsunami of snow bore down on me as I continued to hasten my speed, but as I looked over my shoulder, I knew there was no way of eluding the Himalayas' rolling ocean.

I was swallowed whole.

I tumbled about like a rag doll, completely consumed and suffocated by the heavy white powder of death, which had dispelled my snow angels and replaced it with a monster. I couldn't fight it. I couldn't escape from it. I was helpless to the monster's claws.

"I'll be with Rob in no time," I told myself.

That was the only thing keeping me going as I suffered inside of the devastating avalanche. *I might as well use the sliding snow to my advantage.*

I closed my eyes and left my body as it was thrown to the bottom of the other side of the mountain. I felt much lighter in the snowy maelstrom. I left behind the clowns, the fear-sniffing dogs, Mr. Henderson, my burst appendix, the 72nd floor, and now the Himalayan Mountains.

I couldn't wait to tell Uncle Ricky.

I hiked the Himalayas.

15

THE BEGINNING

I came full circle.

Well, almost.

It was more like an ellipse.

During my entire journey, the two parallel loci points of the ellipse were like a pair of weathered fingers outstretching a rubber band that was moments away from snapping due to extreme pressure.

"Hello," I muttered, my voice echoing off the houses. "Is there anybody here?"

The two loci points, the beginning and end of my journey, were one and the same all along. Finally, the fingers testing the rubber band's flexibility relaxed and met each other in the middle of the empty space defining the band's region of interest to form a single mid-point ... my home.

"If you go looking for your own heart's desire," I chanted, "and you can't find it in your own backyard, then you've never really had it at all."

I walked up Florence Court and into the middle of the cul-de-sac like Dorothy taking her final steps on the yellow brick road back toward Kansas.

"Home sweet home," I said. "I was here all along. Rob was here all along."

I sensed his presence. He was within my grasp.

"I never had to look for him inside the shed," I realized.

I should have listened to Jeff and Mike when they tried to prevent me from leaping over the moat surrounding the shed. Rob was right under my nose, and I never had to go on a wild goose chase amidst my most wicked nightmares in search of my condemned brother. I hiked a million miles to travel three feet.

"Or did I?"

As I circled my childhood cul-de-sac, where an overwhelming sense of joyous nostalgia suddenly came over me, I narrowly escaped the unmapped cul-de-sac of my subconscious where the stench of my fears emanated for all of my monsters and barriers to trace and exploit. However, as I left one cul-de-sac and entered another, I noticed nothing but similarities between the two dead ends.

"Where is everybody?"

I was expecting Jeff or Mike to come running out of their house to join me in the street for a game of wiffle ball. I was expecting to hear Mom call me in for lunch. But nobody was there to greet me. I was alone.

Something didn't feel right. The block was cold and quiet.

A light dusting of morning frost coated the lawns. The timers to the houses' Christmas lights and decorations had long expired all around the cul-de-sac as the rising sun issued natural light along the horizon.

"I did come full circle," I asserted. "It's Christmas morning."

I embraced my brother's Christmas gift, still unaware of what was inside. I hoped that it wasn't too late to give it to him on behalf of the mysterious benefactor.

Florence Court was deserted. Usually the street was hopping with life, but as I stood under the darkened street lamp holding a Santa Claus patterned box on what I suspected was Christmas morning, I feared that all of the life had been sucked out of my childhood home. I had always thought that the cul-de-sac would preserve the spirit of my childhood in a timeless vacuum, but the air in that vacuum had turned sour in my death, and the lifelessness was smothering me.

My solitude reminded me of my final years living on this block. All alone. I was waiting for my childhood to come running out of the neighborhood houses, but only the cold breeze of loneliness whipped me in the face. Jeff and Mike had moved on. Rob was in college. I was surrounded by the houses, mailboxes, the inactive basketball hoops, and the second base tree in Jeff and Mike's backyard that reminded me of my fleeting youth, as well as the friends and family that I used to share it with.

Everybody was gone, again, and I was trapped underneath the street lamp scraping the paved road for the hidden layers of my past where the essence of life inhered in the coveted skid marks and road bumps.

"The green door!" I exclaimed.

My unshakable loneliness was confirmed as I observed the red door on my house turn green. I rubbed my eyes in disbelief.

"It's the green door," I repeated.

◆   ◆   ◆

Another one of the changes affecting my bid at recapturing my childhood was the color of our front door. My entire wonderful youth was marked by a bright red front door accenting our white house of twelve Florence Court at the top of the cul-de-sac. It was a family trademark for years.

Whenever somebody needed directions to the house, like the pizza deliveryman, we would finish off our instructions with, "… and we're the white house with the red door." It was a perfect way to identify and distinguish ourselves from the other families.

After college, however, my Dad decided to paint the red door green, and for me, it marked the end of an era.

There would be no debate as to what the new color of the door was going to be once all of the coats were applied. It wasn't lime green, sea green, forest green, or chartreuse. It was simply green, like right out of a Crayola box, and there were a lot of people, including my mother, who had a hard time adjusting.

Mom fought with my dad for weeks over the new color of the door, and she threatened to paint over his hard work. The three coats of primer and five coats of paint would be covered by an inconspicuous hue if he didn't succumb to her intimidations.

"I see yellow coming through the green," Mom claimed, her hand over her gaped mouth to keep from puking. "It's making me nauseous."

"Yellow?" Dad retorted, disgusted with my mom's fatuous pleas. "There's no yellow. It's a *green* door. Where do you see the yellow?"

"Green is made of yellow and blue," my mom lectured, "and I see the yellow."

"Do you know what you're talking about?" Dad angrily responded.

Mom, deeply offended, marched to the car, stepped into the driver's seat, and slammed the door shut. "I'm going to Home Depot to buy a different color," Mom fumed. "Are you coming with me?"

"No," Dad coldly answered.

Mom's intimidations were not working. Dad wasn't budging.

He was calling her bluff.

"You're going to make me do this by myself," Mom seethed, as she revved the engine to portray her seriousness and urgency.

"Will you relax," Dad urged. "It looks fine."

"When you want to do something, it gets done," Mom yelled, buckling her seatbelt while shifting the car in reverse. "But when I want something done, you're too tired and lazy to do anything. I'm going to Home Depot and you're going to repaint the door today. I can't live in this house with a yellow door. It's making me sick."

Mom slowly backed down the driveway, acting repulsed as she continued to eyeball the green door in search of more things to complain about it. She was playing the guilt game while stalling to give my dad more time to relent to taking a ride with her to the store for a more common, less dramatic color of paint.

"I'm not repainting the door today," Dad retorted.

Mom sped out of the driveway and accelerated down the hill.

I couldn't believe the scene that had just taken place in front of our new-look home; a fight over the color green. I thought I had seen it all. Pointless coats of paint on a meaningless door caused weeks of aggravation.

Has life devolved so much for my parents to warrant such an argument?

A question like that could only be answered in death, from the outside looking in, while searching for the true meaning(s) of life. If the color of our front door represents all that we are, then we would never have any reason to see what's beyond them.

I didn't claw my way through the gates of hell just to change the color of my childhood front door. I came back to knock through it. That was where the true colors of life dwelled. If only we achieved such enlightenment while we were alive, maybe then we wouldn't have wasted so much time worrying and arguing along the way with the doors to life slamming in our faces.

You can paint the door all of the colors of the rainbow, but it still won't improve or enhance the more important space behind that door.

"When Mom gets back," Dad ordered, his patience waning as he washed the paintbrush under a running faucet, "you tell her you like the green."

"I will," I promised.

I promised to lie to my mom. I didn't like the color of the door. If it were up to me, I would have kept it red. Not because the green made me nauseous, but because it symbolized the unstoppable changes occurring all around me. We were no longer the white house with the red door at the top of the hill.

I was lost because I continued to follow the antiquated directions to my home at twelve Florence Court like a carefree child in a desperate search for a red door.

My identity was camouflaged.

Mom returned from her quest for another shade of green shortly after Dad finished cleaning up his workspace. She never went to the store. She drove halfway around the block before making an about-face back into the driveway. She had more to say to my dad, so the arguments over the new color of our front door continued well into the night. I only exacerbated the bickering by reluctantly agreeing with my dad when I was unfairly asked to take sides.

"It looks nice," I lied, envisioning the red door of my childhood.

"You have no sense of design," Mom snapped at me. "Can't you two see the yellow seeping through the door or are you colorblind?

Colorblind, I wondered. *We should only be so lucky.*

I spent most of my time in the middle of the cul-de-sac staring at the green door wishing I could achieve colorblindness. And now, in death, after a harrowing yet essential date with the Himalayan Mountains, I attained that colorblindness.

I never saw so clearly in years.

◆   ◆   ◆

I was home no matter what color the door was at the moment.

"It's not about the door," I told myself. "It's what's behind the door."

I walked toward my house, still discouraged by my solitude, but finally uplifted by the welcoming comfort of my joyous abode. As I made my way over to the driveway, I was immediately attracted to my mailbox. The beautiful bush surrounding the letterbox was brimming with colorful flowers and ample green leaves. However, it smelled intriguingly of burned toast and fried bumblebees. The odor embraced my attentive nostrils with fond memories of the past.

"The burning bush," I remembered.

The small flag attached to the mailbox was raised. I curiously opened the door and reached my hand into the small opening. I didn't expect to find any delivered letters in the mailbox, being that it was Christmas morning, but I sensed that I would uncover something significant to my journey.

I pulled out a perfectly scuffed wiffle ball, which immediately hypnotized my lips and issued a genuine smile across my face.

"I am not alone!" I shouted. "I am not alone!"

I gripped the wiffle ball and spun around in place. The neighborhood Christmas lights simultaneously turned back on and the once desolate houses imposing its lifelessness around the cul-de-sac were now saturated with vivaciousness. I heard the whispers and felt the shadows of my neighbors circling me. I wanted to cry out, "Olly olly oxen free," and reconcile myself with my childhood friends at the cul-de-sac's green electric box where we would be safe from taggers from beyond the grave during our overnight games of Ghost in the Graveyard.

I was close. Really close.

I placed the wiffle ball back into the mailbox and stared up at my house.

I feared that if it was Christmas morning, then there wouldn't be anybody home, and my journey to find my brother would continue on forever. Dad and Mom were probably still at Grandma's sitting around the pile of presents in the extension, arguing over the size of the pile with the rest of the family, waiting impatiently for Rob and me to return before taking down the holy mountain one gift at a time.

They better not start without us, I hoped. I had one more gift to add to the pile before the festivities got underway, and I wanted to be there to watch Rob open it. *Therein lies the rub,* I marveled. *Where the hell is Rob?*

I made a mental checklist recounting all of the unattractive nooks and crannies of hell that I barged through in search of Rob, only to come out empty-handed.

(1) The shed

(2) The road to nowhere

(3) The hospital

(4) The 72nd floor

(5) The Himalayan Mountains

I was running out of places to search.

Or maybe I was searching in the wrong places.

I continued to be drawn to the house, which upon closer inspection as I practiced my baby steps routine, was remarkably impervious to time's decay. The wood facing was washed and dressed for the occasion. The holiday lights welcomed the Christmas season, but the house's inherent shine, which was glowing brightly like a nubile star in the nighttime sky, welcomed my expected visit with open arms. It was calling me as it had so many times before for one final dance.

However, I still couldn't get past the green door. It stood out like a bloody wart on an otherwise flawlessly sculpted replicated statue of David.

I didn't want to find out what was on the other side of the green front door. I was afraid that I would find nothing, nothing at all, resulting in nowhere else to turn.

All of a sudden, the more realistic prospect of actually being reunited with my family was equally terrifying. I didn't know how I should feel any longer, but I didn't travel all this way to stand at the end of the driveway pondering endlessly over my options when, in reality, I had no options at all.

"Okay," I said, trying to talk some sense into myself before mistaking my home for another brothel in hell. "I'll check the house, but then I'll have to find a way to get to Long Island before everybody's finished opening their presents."

I couldn't delay the inevitable. I refused to persistently think myself around in circles until I couldn't discern my left from right ... a red door from a green door ... heaven from hell. Rob was here. I was here. We were home. The journey was over.

I was sure I would be able to come up with a few topics to talk about upon our retarded meeting in the heavenly afterlife.

I owed him an apology.

The sky growled unobtrusively as if urging me to resume my confident pace up the driveway and to my home.

"Thunder!" I yelled excitedly. My eyes lit up to make up for the temporary lack of lightning in the Christmas morning sky.

I knew exactly where Rob was hiding now. I needed to tag him before he ran to the safety of the green electric utility box. Without hesitation, I sprinted to the garage and flipped open the lid to the garage door keypad, my heart racing and my nerves shaking with excitement. I was one electronic code away from unveiling the finish line to an unforgettable journey through heaven.

Heaven.

The thunder grew louder and louder each time I attempted a different permutation of four-digit passwords. I tried almost every combination of numbers, wishing I hadn't forgotten the magic code. The thunder was rooting me on while the sky snapped Polaroid's of my storied finish, but I was not delivering in the clutch.

I couldn't break through the tape. I tried all of the family birthdates, anniversaries, and lucky numbers, but the garage door wouldn't budge.

I closed my eyes and implored myself to think carefully. The thunder grew louder, or nearer, and sounded more like boos than cheers. The sky was also not too happy that it was wasting its film on me while I stalled for more time.

Nothing was coming to me. I cleared my mind and tried one final combination.

It's alive!

The garage door slowly ascended, providing for me a much-anticipated first look at the long sought-after finish line. It was beautiful.

The thunder chimed, reminding me that my search and rescue mission wasn't exactly over even though I survived the indelible human race of hazardous hurdles and landmines. Parked quietly in the garage was my uncle's Cabriolet convertible hibernating for the winter with the top up.

"He loved that car," I mouthed softly for none to hear. "And what did I do to it? Drive it through a guardrail, down a heavily wooded hill, and into a tree."

My set of Titleist golf clubs poked up from the backseat, but they didn't catch my attention. As I had suspected, something was moving in the front passenger's seat. I shuddered from a piercing excitement that could only be absorbed on Christmas morning while standing before the present of a lifetime. It felt like somebody had snuck up behind me and surprisingly dropped a freshly made ice cube down my back.

The sky continued to have a birthday celebration of its own, which leaked through the garage's filthy windows.

"I'm stalling again," I told myself.

I was glad I didn't come across nothing at all. I walked around the car toward the driver's side door and peered through the window.

"There he is," I said. "Right where I expected."

Rob held his head in his hands and nervously rocked back and forth in the passenger's seat. He appeared to be in a state of shock, trying to mentally escape the hell that he was stuck inside.

I knew exactly how he felt.

Rob did not sense my presence. He was too busy traversing his personal road. I surveyed his turmoil behind the safety of the car's glass shield, looking forward to disrupting his disruption. A rumble of thunder rolled over our heads causing my brother to shiver. I heard his cries filter through the window.

He's in the safest place to be during a thunderstorm, I remembered. But I still wanted to save his day. I wanted to yank him from his protective shell and set him free. I wanted to be his superhero ... like Batman.

And then that embarrassing day at the carwash came fluttering back to me like a butterfly to its larvae young; the day I was flanked by both Batman and the Joker, good and evil, in the backseat of my neighbor's newly-washed car, hoping that the glass shields safeguarding my existence didn't come tumbling down without warning, profiting from my vulnerability as I futilely attempted to ward off the struggles of Batman's heaven and the Joker's hell forever … and ever.

"I am Batman," I said to myself, fogging up the driver's side window with my breath, as I continued to watch my brother's unending inability to escape from being stuck in-between his interpretations of good and evil from inside of the car.

It was time.

I opened the door and slid behind the wheel of the car, and for the first time since our fatal car accident, Rob and I were together in my Cabriolet. It was the first time we were together anywhere. It was like old times, just like when we were alive.

We are alive.

Rob still didn't acknowledge my intrusion, so I wrapped my arm around him and placed the mystery Christmas gift, addressed to him, on his lap.

I finally got his attention. He curiously and gently picked his head up, and we stared at each other, both of our eyes saturated in tears for what seemed like an eternity, but were probably only a few seconds.

His, tears of fear and loneliness.

Mine, tears of joy and relief.

My goal was to get Rob to cry my freshly baked recipe because it didn't sting and irritate the eyes nearly as much as his old, played-out concoction did.

All that I suffered to reach this point was worth every inch of heartache because the space between our stares was electric in the moment. Rob looked at me appreciatively as we waited for the storm to pass together. I wanted to tell him all about my journey. I wanted him to know that he didn't have to be afraid anymore.

"I'm sorry," I said, breaking apart the most comfortable silence there ever was between us. He responded with the ingredients to my tears, which finally vindicated me of my sins. It was then that I realized how necessary my journey really was, not for finding my brother, who was safe at home all along, but for discovering myself.

More than anything else, I needed self-vindication and a meaning to my shortened life so I could accept my mortality, more easily overcome the obstacles that I imposed upon myself, and better see the light that is my home.

Rob was that light. He was the lighthouse on the sandy shore courting me while I was in the shed hiding from Mr. Henderson. He shined brightly over the dark tepid seas while my IV lines were caught in the elevator doors at Columbia Presbyterian. He showed me the way and steered me away from evil with his unending 100-mile long glow like the bat signal projected into the night sky. Like the best sailors though, I didn't come to see the lighthouse per se. I came to see the ocean.

Home sweet home.

Once upon a time I was an ocean, I recited.

I remembered walking out to the ocean from my uncle's deck in Sagaponack, which was the perfect metaphor for my long, eventful journey home. Instead of taking the convenient boardwalk connecting the deck with the ocean, I was lost among dunes of sand and grass while searching endlessly for the light to show me the way.

"Merry Christmas," Rob choked, stifling his tears away.

"I brought you a present," I said, pointing to the festively decorated wrapped box on his lap. "Come on, open it up."

I was just as eager to see him open up the present as he was. After carrying it for so long, I still couldn't use my Christmas powers to infer what was inside. Rob's hands shook as he meticulously disrobed the wrapping paper from the box.

Here it is, I anticipated. *The first gift of the season.*

For the first time in a long time, that delightful tingling sensation of family tradition completely invested my being, and all of the magic of Christmas that had once fizzled away as youth gave way to adulthood cascaded back into my encyclopedia of reality.

Rob finally ripped open the box and pulled out his Power Rangers knapsack. He was delighted and I finally sensed that he was going to be okay.

"Your lucky book bag," I said, astounded.

I thought I left it behind in the shed.

Maybe it does hold some mystical powers, I wondered. *Could it have helped me escape Everest's avalanche?*

I was repaying Rob the favor that he unselfishly did for me. After all this time, I was unknowingly my brother's lighthouse directing him home from the lost sand dunes of time because he now appeared to be free from whatever demons that were holding him back from reaching the light.

"Thank you so much," Rob cried, as he attached the bag to his back.

"It's from Grandma," I told him, finally realizing whom it had come from.

I no longer felt the urge to continue apologizing to Rob for not being there for him over the years or for failing to help him against Mr. Henderson in the shed, Mongo on Halloween night, and the park ranger at the golf course. I could have apologized again for firing him and subsequently killing him in the car crash, but I didn't feel like this was the time or place for an apology anymore. Rob and I were together and that was all that mattered.

"Potato chips and iced tea," Rob said.

"What?" I asked.

"My lasts," he continued. "Potato chips and iced tea. That was the last food and drink of my life. At the gas station on our trip upstate."

"Buttered bagel and a Pepsi," I chimed in, as I smiled and laughed with my brother as we reviewed our lasts for the last time.

The thunderstorm was dissolving.

"What do we do now?" I asked my brother.

Our parents were most likely at Grandma's house, and we were celebrating Christmas morning inside a parked car in our childhood garage 100 miles away. The last thing that I wanted to do was start traveling again, even if this time I had a companion for the ride.

Rob contemplated my question, looked at me sternly, and opened the car door. "Everything," he responded. "Let's do everything."

As he exited the car, I heard somebody's footsteps add superfluous strain to the creaky wooden floor right above my head. I jumped up excitedly and fell out of the Cabriolet. That sound could only be made by one house.

And then I heard another unique sound bleeding through the walls.

> *As soon as you realize you notice the light,*
> *Free to be selfish, you've earned the right,*
> *Succumb to the struggle, the turn of the tides,*
> *Fresh out of wisdom, ahead of one's time.*

Dad was playing his music, and as I listened through the poor acoustics of the garage, I finally understood all of his lyrics.

"They're home!" Rob screamed passionately. He took his shoes off and opened the door that led inside. A bright light shone through the doorway. Rob looked back at me and smiled as he stepped in. "Come on," Rob urged. "Everybody's here and the Christmas pile is bigger than ever."

The outside of the house may have been my childhood home, but the inside was most definitely my grandmother's, and like my brother noted, everybody was within the vessel spreading Christmas cheer.

"Are you coming?" Rob asked. He was impatiently waiting for me to join him. "I smell monster meat." He stepped into the light and disappeared.

"Wait for me!" I shouted.

I ran over to the door, took off my shoes, and stepped into the doorway as the white light slowly enveloped me.

"Merry Christmas!" I hollered into the house. I smiled, disappeared into the light, and shut the door behind me.

Home sweet home.
It was as if I never left.

978-0-595-43748-1
0-595-43748-6

Printed in the United States
80908LV00001B/52-75